THE EDINBURGH SKATING CLUB

A Note on the Author

Michelle Sloan trained as a primary school teacher and studied drama and arts journalism. She is the author of several books for children. *The Edinburgh Skating Club* is her debut adults' novel. Originally from Edinburgh, Michelle now lives in Broughty Ferry with her family.

The
Edinburgh Skating Club

Michelle Sloan

First published in 2022 by Polygon,
an imprint of Birlinn Ltd.

Birlinn Ltd
West Newington House
10 Newington Road
Edinburgh
EH9 1QS

www.polygonbooks.co.uk

1

This is a work of fiction.

ISBN 978 1 84697 595 0
eBook ISBN 978 1 78885 520 4

A catalogue record for this book is available on request
from the British Library.

Typeset by Initial Typesetting Services, Edinburgh

For Kay and Karen, with much love

Chapter 1

18th century, Edinburgh

It was, considered Mrs Alison Cockburn as she strode across the cobbled streets, increasingly difficult to traverse Edinburgh's Old Town without trailing one's skirts in 'nastiness'. She looked up to the unusually clear blue skies, punctured by the gleaming spire of St Giles' Cathedral, and was about to take a deep breath of the smoky, autumnal air when she plunged her right foot into the familiar warmth of a heap of malodorous, steaming horse manure.

She shut her eyes momentarily and let out a long groan. 'Intolerable!'

'Aye, but at least it's from a horse,' said a passing man, with a smirk.

Mrs Cockburn raised an eyebrow. It was true: the contents of a chamber pot were no longer to be hurled from upper windows during the daytime. Grimacing, she hoisted her skirts and withdrew her foot, examining what now clung to her shoe. No patten could have won the battle against such a gargantuan pile of nastiness, even had she worn the devilish clicking things; they had been thrown out after one attempt at walking on cobbles.

Glancing around, she raised her heavy skirts to well above an 'appropriate' level, gave the petticoat layers a tarantella-like swoosh to remove the last of the filth, and, pulling her shawl firmly around her forearms, continued on her way.

As she approached the town's spine, the Royal Mile, the noise and smells intensified. Around her the good folk of Edinburgh loitered and gossiped while children played at their feet in the dirt, and ruddy-armed washerwomen pegged out their linen on criss-crossed lines in the narrow closes. Shrieking gulls swooped undeterred by the street vendors and shopkeepers who bellowed and shook their fists at the flying robbers. Laughter, shouts and swirling voices caught on the putrid wind as Alison Cockburn turned and headed up the Lawnmarket towards the castle. Cramped, overcrowded and dingy, Edinburgh's Old Town was no longer a desirable neighbourhood and the gentry were leaving in their droves, heading across the drained ditch that had once been the cesspit of the Nor' Loch to the space and symmetrical neatness of the New Town.

Almost at Castlehill now, Mrs Cockburn noticed a large cart piled high with trunks and boxes at the mouth of the close known as James Court, and as she turned down the wynd she saw that a line of aproned footmen were passing items hand to hand to be loaded on to the cart. She navigated her way down to the other end and saw that the human chain was snaking its way from the very doorway she was intending to enter.

'Be careful with that lantern, young man!' shouted a voice from above. 'Ah, Mrs Cockburn. What a delight to see you!' Mrs Cockburn looked up at the rotund face of her friend peering from a window some three storeys up.

'Good morning, Mr Hume!' she called back. 'I see I have come visiting at a most inopportune time.'

'Indeed, Mrs Cockburn, we are in a state of chaos . . . Do be careful with that!' he snapped suddenly as two footmen staggered into view from the doorway below him carrying a heavy wooden chest. 'As you see, Mrs Cockburn, today we leave the slum.'

Alison Cockburn rolled her eyes. 'I see, Mr Hume. Paradise awaits you, does it so?'

'Paradise indeed, Mrs Cockburn. They say St Andrew's Square is quite heavenly.'

'Choirs of angels will herald your arrival, I have no doubt,' replied Mrs Cockburn with a wry smile. 'And how will you write about human nature, Mr Hume, when all you observe are angels?'

At this, her friend let out a bellowing laugh that echoed around the high walls of the courtyard, causing the footmen to look up in surprise.

'You and your dear sister will never want to associate with your devilish acquaintances from this side of town again.'

Another figure appeared at the window beside Hume, a woman with the same round cheeks as her brother and ringlets framing her face. She was clutching to her bosom a small, rust-coloured and extremely fluffy dog, which was panting so excitedly it looked as though it were smiling.

'Not a bit of it, Mrs Cockburn,' said Katherine Hume. 'You must come and see us often.'

'Good morning to you, Miss Hume. And Foxey too.'

Hearing his name, Foxey's ears pricked and he looked at Mrs Cockburn below. Unfortunately, he also caught sight of a cat lying in a patch of sunlight, its tail flicking angrily. Foxey shot out of his mistress's arms like a ball from a musket and disappeared into the house.

'Oh Lord,' said Katherine Hume. 'Foxey's seen the cat. Catch him, brother!'

'That is the second time this week!' hollered Mr Hume. 'Katherine, my dear, this is too much.'

'I told you to keep the door closed.'

Their bickering continued as Mrs Cockburn looked at the main door. 'Can't we just shut the one down here?' she said, and was about to kick the doorstop out of the way when a flash of orange fired out of the passageway. The cat let out a yowl and bolted up the close with Foxey on its heels.

'Catch him!' yelled Mr Hume, now very red-faced and wringing his hands. 'For pity's sake, catch him, Mrs Cockburn. Save him before he's snatched and skinned and his pelt turned into a fine lady's muff.'

Alison Cockburn groaned for the second time that morning before dropping her shawl, hoisting her skirts up once again, and hurrying back up the close towards the Lawnmarket. She pushed her way out on to the busy main street and caught a fleeting glimpse of Foxey in full cry racing down the hill.

There was nothing for it: she would have to run.

Chapter 2

'I must say, Mrs Cockburn,' said Mr Hume, standing to carve a thick slice of venison from a handsome joint, 'I was very impressed with your commitment to catching our beloved little friend.'

They were sitting in the dining room of the Humes' elegant abode in the New Town. The ceilings were decadently high and appointed with the finest cornicing, the windows long and draped in rich damask curtains. But despite the cheerful flames in the marble fireplace it was draughty and chilly, and so Mrs Cockburn had kept a shawl wrapped neatly around her shoulders. Instead of the usual drunken, night-time bellowing that could be heard in the Old Town at this hour, there was only the gentle clop of horses' hooves on the quiet streets.

Mr Hume continued, 'And your athleticism is quite astounding – for a woman.'

Mrs Cockburn noticed a sideways glance from Katherine, a trace of a smile on her lips. She reached for her wine glass and took a sip of the claret, casting her mind back to the calamitous experience of chasing at full pelt down the High Street after Foxey, who in turn had been hell bent on catching the blasted cat. With her skirts and petticoats bunched up, exposing her stockings, she had, at times, on the steeper stretches completely lost control, managing to knock over an apple cart and scatter several unsuspecting chickens; she had slid through countless piles of nastiness, barely managing to regain her balance as she tripped over uneven cobbles, and had come close to a head-on collision with two footmen carrying a sedan chair before finally catching up with the panting Pomeranian in the kirkyard, the cat nowhere to be seen.

Foxey had seemed delighted, and possibly relieved, to see her. And there they had flopped, recovering together amongst the dead – both considering what had just occurred, and wondering what the aftermath might look like on their return journey to James Court. Now, reflecting on her adventure, 'athleticism' was not, she thought, quite the word that sprang to mind. She swallowed her wine.

'Indeed?' she said smoothly. 'In truth, I was aware of movement in parts of my anatomy that have never moved before.' A snort escaped her, and Katherine reached for her handkerchief and clamped it over her mouth, her eyes shut tight, her shoulders shaking. Mr Hume paused in his carving and stared at his sister.

'Why, dear sister, are you in some sort of discomfort?' he said. 'Are you choking?

'I do not understand what ails you both. I watched you dash up that close, Mrs Cockburn, as nimble as a young lad – as though your very life depended on saving dear Foxey!'

'You are very kind, Mr Hume,' said Mrs Cockburn, drying her eyes with her napkin and attempting to steady herself, 'to compare my sudden and somewhat maniacal burst of energy in such Panglossian terms. I can assure you that if you were to discuss it with the good tradespeople who found themselves in my way, they certainly would not describe my movements so favourably.'

Mr Hume shook his head in confusion and returned to sawing the joint. 'Well,' he said, 'Foxey is most grateful to you, as are Katherine and I. I do recall perhaps your looking a little troubled when you returned – your attire somewhat rearranged.'

At this, Katherine was off again.

Mrs Cockburn looked down to the floor, where Foxey sat gazing up at her with adoration . . . or was it hope that she might drop a sliver of ham from her fork into his jaws?

'I must say,' she said, 'I thoroughly enjoyed the whole experience. It was quite exhilarating.'

'Interesting. How so, Mrs Cockburn?' said Mr Hume.

Mrs Cockburn placed her knife and fork on her plate and considered. 'The speed of movement, the rush of the sharp autumnal air in my face.'

'Indeed?' said Mr Hume with genuine interest.

'But, dear brother,' said Katherine, 'by saying "for a woman", were you not implying that Mrs Cockburn's athleticism must necessarily be less than a man's?'

'Well said, Katherine,' interjected Mrs Cockburn. 'When, for that matter, did you last witness any male display of athleticism, Mr Hume?'

David Hume momentarily pushed his lips out so that, with his large cheeks and big, glassy eyes, he had the appearance of a bloated fish. He stroked his chin, and then, quite suddenly, his face broke into a broad smile. He raised a finger to the air.

'I know exactly when I saw an impressive display of outstanding athleticism from not one man but several fine gentlemen. Last winter, when I was invited to witness the Edinburgh Skating Club in action at Duddingston Loch.'

'Athleticism?' said Katherine. 'Come now, brother. Balance and poise, yes, but surely no athleticism.'

'Forgive me, but you are quite wrong, dear sister – and you weren't there,' replied Hume, with a twinkle in his eye. 'Balance and poise are indeed essential, but in terms of athleticism there was stamina, strength and at times quite impressive speed. They jump and leap and perform all number of quite exhausting feats.'

'It sounds wonderful. I should offer my services. Ah! But no! As you have so rightly pointed out, I am a woman,' said Mrs Cockburn with a smile. 'That door is firmly closed, as are those of all the other societies. Let me see. Here in our city we have the Speculative Society, the Lunar Society, the Arts Society, the Celtic Society, the Philosophical Society, the Oyster Club . . .'

Mr Hume chewed and nodded at each one.

'. . . the Dialectic Society, the Select Society . . .'

'Don't forget the Cape Club, the Poker Club, the Crochallan Fencibles and the Easy Club,' added Katherine.

'Yes!' said Mrs Cockburn, raising her glass in agreement. 'One wonders if the gentlemen of Edinburgh are ever at home.'

'I take your point, Mrs Cockburn,' said Mr Hume. 'And if I could make it so, I would have you as a member of all these societies. With your wit, intelligence and indeed your athleticism you would make a fine addition.' He smiled, and stabbed at a potato on his plate, popping it into his mouth.

'Perhaps Mrs Cockburn should do just that,' said Katherine.

'And how do you propose she manages that, dear

sister?' chuckled Hume. 'Would you have her pose as a man?'

Katherine raised her eyebrows and looked at Mrs Cockburn. 'My dear brother said himself that you looked as "nimble as a young lad".'

Mrs Cockburn once again began to chuckle.

'Katherine, what are you suggesting?' said Mr Hume, looking shocked.

'Is this a dare, Miss Hume?' said Mrs Cockburn, loading her fork with asparagus.

Katherine smiled. 'I do believe it is,' she said.

Chapter 3

21st century, Edinburgh

The image on the screen was a painting of a man dressed in full Highland dress. He gazed back at the undergraduates in the lecture theatre with nonchalant disdain, dark clouds brooding behind him.

'Consider the boldness of his expression, the dramatic lighting, the vitality, indeed the spontaneity of the brushstroke; there's a striking realism of character. Seeing these paintings you already feel you know the sitters. This was Raeburn's indisputable skill, and what made him not only Enlightenment Edinburgh's most sought-after portrait painter but an essential component, the visual representation if you will, of that particular period. Not only was he part of the cultural movement, but he captured it and recorded it in the genius of his painting.'

Somewhere in the room a phone began buzzing like an angry bee. There was a general shifting as several students began frantically rummaging in their bags. Everyone else sat with eyes glazed.

Claire Sharp sighed. 'Don't worry about it,' she said with a wave of her hand. 'To be honest, that's the last slide.' She clamped her thumb on the remote, ending the lecture. The lights came up and the roomful of bodies leapt into life.

'Essays are due in in two weeks,' she heard herself drone over the noise, 'and with the end of the semester looming – and, of course, exams – you should keep on top of everything.' She knew she sounded boring. She felt boring as she said it. They were bored and she was bored. She snapped shut the lid of her laptop and watched as the students began grabbing their jackets, chatting and moving down the stairs to leave the room. No one said anything; a few faces smiled weakly in her general direction but most just looked delighted to be escaping. Claire knew how they felt. Within a couple of minutes, the lecture theatre was empty. She reached for her coat and began packing up her bag. The buzzing bee began again. Claire tutted and reached into the bag to retrieve her phone. There were two missed calls. It must have been *her* phone vibrating. She swiped her finger across the screen, feeling relieved that she hadn't berated her students.

'Hello,' she said.

'Hi, Dr Sharp, it's Liz from Abercrombie and Murray here. Just to say the couple who visited your flat on Sunday have decided not to make an offer after all. They say they've seen something else more suitable, I'm afraid.'

'Hmm,' said Claire, sinking down into a chair. 'But they seemed really keen. They *were* really keen. That was their second visit and they practically begged me to tell them what I wanted for it.'

There was a pause.

'That's just the way things go, I'm afraid,' said Liz eventually. 'I'll keep you posted if there's any more interest in a viewing. Bye for now.'

'Oh, okay,' said Claire. Did that mean she would have to keep doing open viewing twice a week, too? 'Actually, Liz—'

It was too late. She'd gone.

'Bugger, bugger, bugger,' muttered Claire.

'Rehearsing another riveting lecture, Dr Sharp?' said a voice at the door. A small woman, laden down with plastic bags straining under the weight of several books, wandered into the room.

'Very funny, Jen.' Claire stood up to resume packing her bag.

'Bad day?' said her friend.

'Just, you know, stuff,' said Claire. 'What are you doing here anyway?'

'I thought maybe you'd like to go for a drink?'

Claire twisted her mouth into a smile. 'On a school night, professor?'

Jen raised her eyebrows. 'I *think* we're allowed to do these things now we're grown up, but if you want to phone your mum first?'

'Very funny,' said Claire, but then she traced the alternative in her mind: the cramped bus journey home, the trudge through the gloomy grey streets and then the stairwell of her tenement flat, opening the door to emptiness. Another lonely night in. This, or a convivial evening with Jen and the journey home cushioned in the glow of red wine.

'Okay,' she said. 'Might be nice to moan at you for a bit.'

Just then her phone began to vibrate again. It was a voicemail message.

'Let me just get this,' she said to Jen. 'My phone was ringing mid-lecture.' She rolled her eyes, and wriggled her arm into her coat. 'It's probably just the estate agent again, telling me that my flat will never, ever, ever sell.' She tapped the screen and pressed the phone to her ear. But it wasn't Liz.

The voice was quiet and slow. 'Dr Sharp, my name is Peter. I'd like to have a chat with you about an opportunity that might be of interest to you. I can assure you it will be well paid. I'd be grateful if you could call me back.'

Claire frowned. 'That's a bit weird,' she said. She played the voicemail again, this time on speaker, turning the volume up. She didn't know anyone called Peter. She didn't recognise the voice, which was neutral, with no strong accent – educated but not posh.

'An "opportunity"?' said Jen, still standing by the door. 'Is it a wind-up?'

Claire shrugged. 'It's a bit too odd for that. I mean, it doesn't make sense for just a wind-up.'

'Well, then, you'd better call him back,' said Jen. 'I'll head off to the pub and meet you there. The Beehive okay?' She made for the door and disappeared, leaving Claire alone, frowning at her phone.

'Okay,' she called after Jen. 'I don't know if I *should* call him back. I mean, it could be a scam, couldn't it?' But Jen had gone, and so, reluctantly, she hit the call back button.

'Dr Sharp?' It was the same voice.

'Hello? Yes, is that Peter?' said Claire. 'Look, I got your message. Sorry, but do I know you?'

'Dr Sharp, let me explain. I need an expert to under-take some research,' said the voice.

Claire frowned. 'I see,' she said slowly. 'What kind of research?'

'It would be much easier to tell you in person. Would you be able to meet me tomorrow at the National Gallery, by the Skating Minister. It's time things were put right. I'll be there at one. You don't have any lectures or tutorials at that time, I believe.'

'Meet you? What? Look, this is all a bit too cloak and dagger for my liking,' said Claire with a nervous laugh. 'And how on earth do you know my timetable? And as I don't know you, how will I know who you are?'

'I'll see you there, Dr Sharp. Don't worry about recognising me. I know who *you* are.'

Then Peter hung up.

Claire took the phone from her ear and stared down at the screen. She shook her head as her mind raced. What on earth was that all about? But then one thought surfaced very clearly in her mind: she really needed that glass of wine.

Chapter 4

The door to the National Gallery swung open and the doorman on the other side gave Claire a polite smile. She entered the reception area with the most bizarre sense of trepidation. She had walked through these doors more times than she could count, not only as an art historian, but also as a student and as a child, skipping in clutching her dad's hand. She had dragged him to the same paintings over and over again. Her favourites – Gainsborough's *The Honourable Mrs Graham* and Velázquez's *An Old Woman Cooking Eggs* – were as familiar and as comforting as members of her own family. But of course her most visited, studied and loved was *The Reverend Robert Walker Skating on Duddingston Loch*, attributed on the small card underneath to Sir Henry Raeburn.

But rather than the lovely feeling of homeliness she

usually felt on her arrival, today her stomach lurched and her red-wine head throbbed as she walked through the main halls of the gallery. It had been Jen who had persuaded her to come. Claire had initially wanted nothing to do with Peter. But over their glass, or rather bottle, of wine, things had been said and discussed that had made her re-evaluate the situation. Most pointedly, Jen's eyes had widened to the size of dinner plates at the suggestion of a clandestine meeting in an art gallery in front of an iconic painting. It was too exciting to turn down, she had said. Then she had continued by suggesting that Claire really didn't have anything else quite so stimulating in her life right now. Which was disturbingly true. She *was* going through an existential crisis of boredom, professionally and possibly personally too. And then came the old clincher: *what did she have to lose?* Again, true. Jen had then pointed out that really, how dangerous could it be meeting someone in such a public place with CCTV everywhere? And for goodness' sake, it wasn't going to be anything *dangerous* anyway. Was it?

That was just so typical of Jen. Anyway, it was too late now: curiosity had claimed its victory. She took a deep breath, trying to settle her nerves, plunged her hands deep into her coat pockets and strode onwards as the critical eyes of a hundred portraits bored into her. *What the hell are you doing, you silly middle-aged woman?* they seemed to be saying. *Get a grip—*

'Dr Sharp.'

Claire froze and turned to face the voice.

Could this person really be Peter?

'Forgive me,' he said. 'I saw you arrive and just thought I'd grab you here, rather than at the painting. I'm Peter.' He held out a hand, which she automatically shook. It was like shaking a damp facecloth.

Claire stared and tried to focus her befuddled head. He was nothing like the image she'd created in her mind. First of all, he was very small, and very thin, and he wore an anorak that looked straight out of Marks & Spencer's boys' department from twenty years ago. Yet he was incredibly young. He couldn't have been much over twenty. Did he even shave? On the phone, he had sounded older and more authoritative than his physical appearance suggested. In fact, in the flesh, he was quite, well, underwhelming. Claire found herself feeling almost disappointed.

'Oh, hello. How did you know it was me?' she added, glancing around.

'You have a picture on the university website,' said Peter.

'Right. Yes,' said Claire, feeling completely ridiculous all of a sudden. 'Of course.' So he hadn't been stalking or tracking her every movement. 'And my timetable?'

'Your what?'

'My timetable – you seemed to know when all my classes and tutorials were.'

'Oh, that was just a case of a phone call to the academic office. They were very obliging.'

Claire rolled her eyes. Wait till she told Jen that.

'Right, so now that I know you're not going to put a gun to my back, what can I do for you?' she said.

Peter laughed. 'Goodness me, Dr Sharp. I'm not going to do anything like that. But do come with me.'

They walked together through to the room where, neatly placed in a small alcove against a misty blue wall, hung the painting of the Reverend Robert Walker. Better known as the Skating Minister, this figure was the gallery's poster boy. It was the most iconic image in the collection and had been reproduced on tea towels, scarves, magnets, pens, notepads and T-shirts. It was an image so familiar that it had become almost part of the brickwork. It was because of this familiarity, she had explained to her students, that it presented challenges to a critical examination.

'I read your thesis on Sir Henry Raeburn, Dr Sharp,' said Peter quietly.

'Well, it was written some time ago now.' Claire wondered how old he would have been back then. Three, maybe?

'Let me get straight to the point. The problem of attribution still remains, and it's critical that this is put right,' he said.

'Attribution of the Skating Minister – you mean its not being painted by Raeburn?'

'Of course. You didn't mention that in your thesis, Dr Sharp.'

'No, well, it wasn't the focus of my work.' Claire knew she sounded a little churlish. 'But, actually, Peter, my thesis on Raeburn was written long, long before anyone formally raised the suggestion that he hadn't painted it. Before it was X-rayed and so on. And even then it wasn't definitively shown not to be a Raeburn. The jury's still out on that one.'

'But you agree that it isn't one of his?' said Peter, gesticulating towards the man on the ice.

Claire sighed. She stared at the image. It always surprised her students how small it was in the flesh.

The most striking thing she noticed when she looked at it was, quite simply, the biting chill of the scene. You could almost feel it emanating from the canvas. The figure, dressed in dark clothing and wearing a large black hat, was a bold silhouette moving across the ice, beautifully stark against the pale background. The skater looked highly accomplished: this was no spontaneous act, but a well-practised move, his left leg pushed forward, his right in a partial arabesque behind him. His arms were folded confidently in front of his body, his posture upright and bold, jaunty even.

The only splash of warmth came from the red cord on his skates and the pinkish hue on his cheeks. He was such a distinguished-looking fellow, with his black clothing and white neckerchief. Over time the paint had faded, revealing a *pentimento* – an alteration: the hat had been repainted, the artist presumably initially unhappy with its angle.

But was it really a Raeburn? This was the question. It had been bought at auction by the National Gallery in 1949 and had, as its certification, a flimsy hand-typed document – a letter from the Reverend Robert's great-granddaughter supposedly confirming, in her mind at least, its provenance. But there was no record of the painting before 1902, and as Raeburn rarely signed or dated his paintings a case had been made that this particular painting was simply not one of his. At some point in its history, it had been swallowed into Raeburn's oeuvre and there it had stayed.

'The suggestion that it's not a Raeburn is entirely plausible, and intriguing, I can't deny that,' admitted Claire. 'It's no secret that there's a swathe of art historians who agree.'

'Well, I'm glad *you* agree, Dr Sharp,' said Peter. 'A friend of mine feels very strongly that Henri-Pierre Danloux is the true artist of this piece of work and would like it attributed so. Your input is the one he seeks. You are an expert on Raeburn and so your opinion carries significant weight. He is prepared to pay generously for your services.'

Claire looked around. Fortunately, no one was in close proximity. And even if they were, the deadening acoustics kept their voices low.

'That's quite a lot to unpack, Peter,' she said.

'Not really, Dr Sharp,' said Peter. Something about his tone made Claire clench her jaw. 'If you look at it simply,' he continued, 'this painting is not the work of Sir Henry Raeburn. It was painted by another artist. That is the truth, and it needs to be remedied in the attribution.'

'Come on, Peter. It's much more than that, isn't it?' said Claire. 'The implications of its not being a Raeburn run deep. Not just within the confines of this gallery, but for the wider politics of the picture itself.'

Peter smiled. 'As I say, it's simple. It's not a Raeburn. It was painted by a Frenchman. It's in everyone's interest to know the truth, is it not? Why should the people of Scotland believe this image was painted by one of their own when we know it was not?'

Claire stared at him. 'Who is your friend, Peter?'

He smiled. 'Just an enthusiast.'

'Of Danloux?'

'Of the truth, Dr Sharp,' he said quietly. 'Of the truth.'

Chapter 5

18th century, Edinburgh

Walking across the newly opened North Bridge from the Old Town of Edinburgh, with its cramped and creaking tenements, to the elegant architecture of the New Town, where there was clean air to breathe, Alison Cockburn considered how she might truly 'become' a man. It was all very well dressing as one, but there were, of course, many other aspects of a man's physical presence, manner and attitude to consider if the enterprise were to be a success. And it *was* to be a success. Why, she considered, was she taking up this gauntlet? Perhaps it was simply a case of her age – there was a sense of ennui setting in and the challenge might just pull her from the apathy that had engulfed her in recent years.

Alison was no stranger to the habits of men. She had, after all, been married to one for many years and had a son too, so copying their mannerisms surely wouldn't be too difficult.

She began to observe, as she walked, the many forms of masculinity that surrounded her. There were, of course, differences in shape – tall, short, pudgy and portly, slim and reedy. A man in a rich pea-green coat strode past and Alison observed his style of walking: confident, long step and an upright posture. He tipped his hat as he passed someone of his acquaintance. Even Alison, always happy to walk at a rapid pace, couldn't keep up, but that could have been because her voluminous underskirts caught in bunches between her legs if she walked too fast.

At the foot of North Bridge, she turned in to the serenity of Princes Street and was walking towards the Humes' flat in St Andrew's Square when she saw Katherine coming towards her.

'Why, Katherine,' she said, 'I was about to call upon you.'

'Yes, I know,' said Katherine, slightly out of breath. Her eyes were sparkling with excitement. 'But I decided to come out to meet you. I have a wonderful surprise for you.'

Alison smiled. 'Well, do tell me, dearest,' she said. 'I am all ears!'

'I shall lead the way,' said Katherine, walking past her friend, who turned to follow her back the way she had come, heading to the end of the North Bridge and entering Shakespeare Square. 'We have an appointment at the Theatre Royal!'

'An appointment?' said Alison. 'You don't mean we're to attend the matinee? I rather think we're several hours too early.'

'No, no, no.' Katherine shook her head, her ringlets flinging out to either side, and bustled towards the theatre, where she knocked on a small red door at the side. 'The stage door,' she whispered to Alison, her eyes gleaming. 'We have an appointment,' she leaned in conspiratorially, 'with none other than the distinguished actor Samuel Foote.'

'How intriguing. But, my dear Katherine, why?' said Alison, also in a whisper.

'To turn you into a man, of course!' said Katherine. She knocked again on the door, this time a little more forcefully. Alison didn't have time to react, as just at that moment an upstairs window opened and an enormous pouf of powdered white hair appeared, presumably a periwig of sorts, and attached to it was a face peering down at them.

'Is that you, Miss Hume and companion?'

It was a man's deep, booming voice. His face was painted white, with dramatically arched slug-black eyebrows, and his cheeks and lips were daubed with cherry-red rouge.

'Indeed, Mr Foote? Is that you?' Katherine called back, her voice light and tinkly.

Alison looked from the apparition above them to the red face of her friend, who was trying to stifle her giggles.

'You'll have to excuse me,' said Mr Foote, trying to balance the wig. Some feathers floated down. 'I'm rehearsing the part of Lady Pentweazel. If you don't mind my appearance, please do come in.'

'A little bit of rouge doesn't frighten us, Mr Foote,' said Alison. She turned the handle of the door and they stepped into the passageways of the theatre.

'Oh, how exciting,' said Katherine. 'The smell, the magic . . .' She was peering round every corner, as if she might see something spectacular.

'Upstairs, my dear ladies,' boomed the voice once more. 'Come, join me in the boudoir.'

They worked their way up the narrow staircase and into a spacious room that was packed to the ceiling with clothes, wigs and shoes. And in the middle of it all, wearing the most enormous court mantua, almost as wide as the room itself, was Samuel Foote.

'When one is wearing such a dress it's rather difficult to move. You must forgive me, ladies,' he said, bowing a little and giving a flourish of his plump fingers. Not only was the gown ridiculous, but the wig on his head was as large and heavy as the skirt was wide. He seemed glued to the spot, attempting to keep his head and neck erect under the elaborate hair, complete with fruit and a sailing ship, which was weighing him down. Great sweeping ostrich feathers adorned the very top of the pouf, and every time he as much as shifted his eyes small fronds seemed to come loose and waft to the ground.

Katherine and Alison stood awkwardly, and both gave small nods.

'What a remarkable garment,' said Alison, after a long pause. She then became aware that Katherine was clasping a kerchief to her mouth beside her. She looked at her, but Katherine waved a hand, her face puce, and Alison realised that her friend was rendered incapable of speech because she was laughing so much. She was utterly consumed. Tears rolled down her cheeks. Alison gave her a nudge. 'Oh dear, Mr Foote. Miss Hume is quite overcome,' she said dryly.

But instead of being offended, the actor seemed to be enjoying the reaction and began to move around the room in a most feminine way, fluttering his eyelashes, fanning an invisible fan, and delicately twisting his hammy wrists.

'Dear ladies,' he said in a high-pitched voice, 'take a

turn with me. But don't get too close. I do believe my great periwig is crawling with lice!'

At this, Katherine almost collapsed to the floor, and Alison too began to chuckle. 'This is all terribly amusing,' she said. 'But do you mind my asking how you are going to show me how to walk like a gentleman?'

'Oh, come now, don't get your drawers in a twist,' said Foote, his voice even higher than before. He grabbed both ladies by the hands and began to attempt to dance up and down the room, which only made Katherine laugh harder. As the dance became more and more frantic, Foote lost his balance, tripped on the hem of his colossal dress and landed with his feet in the air, at which point his wig toppled to the side of his head and his foot fell off with a crash.

There was a breathless silence. Then: 'You appear to have lost your foot,' said Alison, holding in her hand a wooden prosthetic which was more than just a foot. It was an entire lower left leg.

'Why, Mr Foote!' cried Katherine. 'You're legless!'

'Well! No wonder I was having trouble dancing,' exclaimed Foote.

Chapter 6

'No, no, no!'

Samuel Foote rapped his stick on the floor impatiently, and Alison Cockburn sighed.

'What have I done wrong this time?' she said. She was standing on the stage of the Theatre Royal, with Katherine perched on one of the seats in the front row of the darkened auditorium. Mr Foote had removed the mantua and was dressed once more as himself, in sacking cloth tunic and breeches. His prosthetic leg had been reattached and in his hand he held the stick which he relied upon to help him maintain his balance, but also used to express his frustration. The stage was set with props and furniture to look like a grand parlour, with two large 'paintings' propped up on stands. It was a scene from the latest comedy, *Taste*, featuring the rather preposterous Lady Pentweazel.

'Watch me again, my dear,' said Foote.

Alison raised an eyebrow.

Foote took a deep, dramatic breath and then walked purposefully across the stage, the wooden leg creating a rather lopsided stride. With his breast puffed out, shoulders broad and wide, and his head held high, the effect was exaggerated and extremely comical. But Alison could detect that amusement would not be welcome any more and so resisted the strong urge to laugh, managing to turn it into a cough.

'Now, your turn,' said Foote, trying to sound encouraging. 'Perhaps, if I may be so bold as to suggest a light bounce in your gait?'

Alison set off once more, but she could feel herself thinking out each step. The bounce made it almost a gallop, and most definitely not a natural walk for a woman, let alone a man.

Foote shook his head in desperation.

'Your posture just doesn't seem quite right,' said Katherine from her seat.

'Two things,' said Alison. 'First, I wish to walk like a man merely strolling along Princes Street, not an actor strutting on a stage. And, second, you must understand, Mr Foote, it is hard to walk like a man when one is wearing a dress. You of all people should know this, given that but an hour ago you were wearing a rather impressive gown yourself.'

Foote sucked in his cheeks and began nodding furiously. 'Quite right, quite right,' he said, and then yelled off stage, 'Smellie!'

A small, stooped man appeared from the depths of the wings. He was wearing an ankle-length jute apron and his greasy hair was tied at the nape of the neck. His face was covered in bulbous growths, and folds of skin fell concertina-like from his chin.

'You called?' he enunciated.

'Smellie, you foul-tempered egg,' said Foote, barely looking at the scowling creature, who stood with his arms folded, 'find this lady a fine gentleman's outfit.'

Smellie glared at Alison. He walked over and re-garded her closely, clearly calculating her size. 'A hat too?' he enquired.

'Well, of course a hat, you imbecile,' said Foote. 'Get to it!'

Smellie walked off the stage, saluting as he passed Foote and muttering, 'Whatever you say, Puff-guts.'

There was a squeak of laughter from the auditorium.

Foote shook his head in despair.

'He is intolerable,' he said into the darkness. 'But once he was the most mesmerising actor. He played the Fool to my Lear. But as himself, he is a gargoyle.' Then he snapped out of his trance and turned once more to face Alison.

'Now, perhaps, 'tis time for us to consider a different

name and a new identity,' he said, walking across the stage to a chair, where he arranged himself artfully, his hand draped over his heart. 'A male persona. A character for you to *become*. Every time you are called Mrs Cockburn, it pulls you back to your feminine ways. We actors have to consider all aspects of our characters, from how they might sneeze to how they take tea or nibble on a piece of ham, or a custard tart.'

'I have never been known to *nibble* anything,' said Alison. 'Rather I scoff urgently, particularly custard tarts.'

Smellie reappeared stage left laden down with garments. He walked over to Alison, dropped them unceremoniously at her feet and gave a low bow. Alison began picking her way through the melee of silk and lace.

'There is a screen backstage,' said Foote, pointing to the far corner of the stage. 'There's a looking glass there too. You do know how to dress yourself in stockings and breeches?'

'I was married for over twenty years,' called Alison, carrying the pile round to the other side of the screen. 'I do know a thing or two about men's clothing.'

There was a small lamp on a table beside the full-length mirror, and she regarded her long frame thoughtfully as she placed the clothes over a chair. She had never been remotely interested in her appearance and had spent as little money as possible on her attire. She wore only simple garments, nothing elaborate or expensive. Practicality had always been her aim. She removed her lace cap and began to rearrange her hair. She undid the braided twist that was neatly pinned at the back of her head and allowed the hair, thinning now and heavily streaked with silver, to hang over her shoulders. Her face, she knew, wasn't particularly handsome. Her features lacked delicacy: her nose was rather long and had a slight bump and her chin protruded, but her cheekbones were high, as was her forehead. And there was undeniably something appealing about her eyes. Her late husband had always remarked on their brightness, and now they twinkled softly back at her from the mirror.

She took off her shawl, shoes and woollen stockings and set about removing her bodice, stomacher and stays, then her skirt, pockets and petticoats. All that remained was her shift, which she decided she would leave on for now, for modesty's sake.

She was a lofty, thin woman and had never been blessed with a voluptuous figure, apart from when she had carried and nursed her son, but now what remained was sagging and shrivelled. She gazed at her silhouette; the faint outline of her breasts still puckered the line of her shift. Perhaps the stays would be enough of a corset to flatten what remained of her bosom. Or would that create too feminine a shaping of her waist? Instead, she experimented by binding her shawl tightly over her shift, wrapping her breasts. She then tied it at the side and tucked in the ends to create a smoother outline. It would do for the moment, until a more suitable alternative could be found. She looked at her reflection once more. Already her posture was more upright. She sat down and pulled on the silk stockings, securing them over her knee with ribbon garters, noticing that her calves, which would now be on display, were pleasingly shapely. She then slipped on the breeches and buttoned them at the front, tucking in her shift. The shoes were high of heel, with metal buckles. She managed to pull on the shirt over her head, but there were no cuff buttons, so she wrapped the ends of the long sleeves around her wrists and held them there as she pushed her arms through the armholes of the waistcoat. This she buttoned up carefully, leaving the collar open so the lacy frills of the shirt would be seen. She tied a cravat under her chin, and a white linen neck-stock would disguise the lack of Adam's apple. Finally, she reached for the jacket, whose mustard-coloured silk matched the waistcoat and breeches.

Fully dressed, she stared at the man looking back at her in the mirror. There was a piece of black ribbon draped over the chair which she now used to secure her hair at the nape of her neck, allowing a long tail to cascade down her back. The few stray whiskers that she had acquired in her fifties now seemed rather distinguished. She pushed her shoulders back and considered what she saw. The outfit was perhaps a little more showy than she would have liked, but the transformation was shocking and impressive. It gave her a stronger frame and a bold silhouette. For the first time in her adult life, Alison Cockburn liked what she saw in the mirror.

She tuned back in to the conversation taking place on the other side of the screen. Foote was regaling his audience with a tale of his theatrical success in Dublin, playing Hamlet, Smellie was interjecting insults whenever he saw an opportunity, and Katherine could be heard calling out questions and chuckling. But then the conversation turned back to her.

'But how on earth do we choose a name?' she heard Katherine ask.

'Smellie, tell us the name of your grandfather on your mother's side,' said Foote.

'Pringle,' snapped Smellie from somewhere in the bowels of the theatre.

'And what was the first name of your schoolmaster when you were but a boy a hundred years ago?' Foote persisted.

'Francis,' called Smellie, his voice trailing into the distance. 'Ye donkey's arse.'

'Francis Pringle!' said Katherine. 'Perfect! What do you say, Alison?'

Alison emerged from behind the screen. 'Francis Pringle at your service,' she said, and gave a full and sweeping bow.

Katherine gasped. Even Foote staggered up from his chair. 'Good gracious,' he said. 'You were born to play a man!'

Katherine appeared out of the gloom of the auditorium, lifting her skirts to run up the steps to join them on stage. Her expression was one of awe and delight. She picked up the hat still sitting on the floor.

'The hat,' she said, a little breathless. 'Try on the hat.' Alison bowed a little so that Katherine could place the hat on her head, then stood up and looked around proudly.

'Well?' she said.

'I rather think you suit the persona of a man almost better than that of a woman,' said Foote. 'As a woman you were – and please don't take this as an insult – rather plain. But as a man you are robust and striking. You appear even to stand and walk like a man now. A romantic hero. And in that outfit you are quite the macaroni!'

'Indeed!' said Katherine, her face lit up. 'I think you will do very well, Mr Pringle.'

'But the question is, will I be recognised as Alison Cockburn?'

Smellie reappeared stage left and silently walked up to Alison. He reached into the large pocket on the front of his apron and produced a small pair of spectacles. 'These are stage props,' he said. 'Just plain glass.' Then, standing on his tiptoes, he carefully placed them on the bridge of her nose. 'Who is Alison Cockburn,' he said, his voice quite unexpectedly dramatic, 'when one is acquainted with Francis Pringle?'

'It is complete!' announced Foote. 'No one would recognise you now. You are reborn!'

'I fear we are weaving a most extraordinary and unpredictable web, Katherine,' said Alison. 'Are we embarking on an adventure too far, dear friend?'

'My dear Pringle,' said Katherine, clasping her hands together, 'what is life without adventure?'

Chapter 7

21st century, Edinburgh

'*H*ow much?'

'You heard me, Jen,' said Claire, lowering her voice.

'Ten thousand?' Jen mouthed the words, then puffed out her cheeks. Claire nodded. They were sitting in the National Gallery café dissecting the meeting Claire had just had with Peter.

'Hard to turn that down,' said Jen, slicing an enormous scone. Then she loaded up her knife with butter from a tiny foil pack and attempted to spread it, cold and hard, on one half. Despite her best efforts, the butter remained in a large unspreadable lump. Undeterred, she smothered on a layer of jam and took a bite, her expression still incredulous.

'So? What did you say?' she said a few moments later, sweeping away crumbs from the table.

Claire took a sip of coffee and rolled her eyes. 'What do you think I said? No, of course.'

Jen nodded thoughtfully. 'Pity though, eh? That money could really come in handy. I'd have been tempted.'

'No, you wouldn't,' said Claire. 'It's completely unethical. I'd lose my job. Not to mention its being somewhat criminal. It would be akin to accepting a bribe.'

'Or would you simply be reinforcing what some of your eminent colleagues have said for some years now?' said Jen. 'Setting the record straight, as it were?'

'Jen, look around you – cast your eyes over the gift shop over there.'

Jen swung round to look at the polished cases and bright lights of the gallery shop. It was simply awash with skating ministers. There was an entire display devoted to the painting. An enormous cardboard cutout of the figure stood at the entrance, and multiple prints and posters hung on the walls depicting the skater in psychedelic Warhol multiples and even as a variety of animals, including a cat and a llama.

Jen looked back at Claire and smiled. 'It's just stuff,' she said. 'People might still buy it, no? I mean it's a nice painting, after all.'

Claire threw up her hands. 'Don't be facetious, Jen,' she said. 'If only it were just stuff. It's a lot more than that and you know it. That painting has become *political*. It's become part of Scotland's identity.'

'Worst-case scenario,' said Jen, now attempting to wedge what was left of the butter on the second half of her scone, 'the gallery has to change the attribution card below the painting. A few people's noses are put out of joint. So what?'

'Do you think that it would happen quietly?' said Claire. 'There would be an almighty furore and massive disagreements amongst experts in the art world. It would affect the value of the painting, and the value of Danloux's work internationally by raising awareness of his name. And no one would agree anyway. They didn't the first time this was suggested.'

'Say you did give it a go, how would you even start?'

'Well, that's just the thing. I'd have to put forward an extremely strong case, including close analysis of some of Danloux's other paintings. I'd then have to persuade the powers that be in this heavyweight institution that they've got it wrong. Imagine how that would go down. I get the feeling that Peter's friend is looking for something more. Some concrete written evidence that makes it unequivocal. Which is like looking for a needle in a haystack. That's a case of trawling through endless historical documents and archives. It's a PhD in itself, actually. And I've got one of those.'

'How did he react, this Peter?' said Jen. 'To you saying *non merci*?'

'Well, I didn't exactly say no. I said I'd think about it,' Claire admitted. 'I'm not good at face-to-face rejection. Anyway, he said he'd give me a ring in a couple of days. I'll give him a definitive no over the phone.'

Jen smiled. 'I suspect he could pick up on the vibes that you weren't going to take the job. In your mind you've said no, so you can return to your quiet existence safe in the knowledge that the Skating Minster stays as a Raeburn and can continue to adorn tea towels across the world. Phew!'

'Mmm,' said Claire. 'I know you're taking the mick.'

'Am I?'

'But I do have another tiny issue.'

'What's that, then?'

'Well, despite everything I've just said, I've always wondered whether it really is a Raeburn,' said Claire.

Jen smiled. 'Ah. Go on – this is intriguing.'

'I've never actually put my doubts into writing, even when I was doing my PhD, as it wasn't the focus of my research. But when the question came up a few years back I wasn't surprised. If you were to line up all the Raeburns in this gallery, the Skating Minster sticks out like a sore thumb. The others are mainly in traditional poses – commissioned portraits. The colours are dark, the faces are rarely in profile and they were all painted in a studio. The minister on ice is an action shot. A moment in time. And it's tiny compared to Raeburn's other figures. In terms of scale, I mean.'

Jen frowned. 'Wait a minute. So you agree with Peter, then?'

Claire shook her head. 'He wants me to convince the world that Danloux painted it. He was a Frenchman who was visiting Edinburgh around the time and who painted, amongst other things, figures in action. There's one in here that has a man in a similar pose to our minister's, except he's a naval officer on a ship, not a skater. Some art historians have argued that this proves Danloux is the true artist, but I can show you some of his precise techniques and styles that just don't add up when it comes to our painting.'

'So, if Raeburn didn't paint it, or this Danloux, then who did?'

Claire smiled. 'Jen, I have absolutely no idea. But this has fired something up inside me. Rather lifts me out of my lethargy. I think I might like to do a little research. Are you in?'

'If it means trips to various art galleries where I can eat scones and jam, then count me in.'

'I think you could take a slightly more active role, Jen. After all, you are a professor of Scottish history,' said Claire with a smile. 'I know you like to forget that.'

'For pity's sake keep your voice down,' said Jen. 'Don't blow my cover as a scone-eating old biddy. Someone might overhear and expect me to actually know stuff!'

Chapter 8

'You can actually see the castle from this room.' Claire took the couple over to the window.

'Oh, how exciting,' said the woman. She peered expectantly out over the rooftops of the gloomy tenements.

'Where?' said her husband.

'Um, if you stand just about here,' said Claire, shuffling over, pointing to the right-hand side of the window. 'And then get up on your tiptoes.'

The couple both obeyed and Claire could see them squinting hopefully, their heads to one side.

'Yes, I think I can see it,' said the woman. 'It's not the best weather today for the views, though, is it?'

Claire smiled weakly. She hoped they hadn't noticed the peeling wallpaper beside the fireplace. And the damp in the cornicing.

'Well, I'll leave you to look around, and if you've got any questions I'll be in the kitchen,' she said.

She folded her arms and sidled out of the room. It was all so irritating – but a necessary evil if she was ever going to sell her flat. She'd been here in Edinburgh's Polwarth area for nearly twenty years. She'd seen businesses nearby come and go. Her beloved local had disappeared, her neighbours changed with the seasons, the terms and now, with the arrival of Airbnb, the weekends. Her son was up and away; she didn't need the extra bedroom, she didn't need the stairwell cleaning hassles, and her knees didn't need the stairs. However, she did need to downsize to free up some cash. She could then help her son and his wife with a deposit for a flat and put some by in case there were more cuts at the university.

She flipped open her laptop and half-heartedly began glancing over the number of first-year essays she still had to mark.

'I think we've seen everything we need to see,' said a voice from the hall. 'We'll let ourselves out.'

'Thanks,' said Claire, standing up to dash out to join them. 'Is there anything else you—'

But they'd gone, the front door swinging shut behind them. She could hear them winding their way down the stairwell, and ran back to the kitchen to peer out of the window until they emerged on to the street and walked away without looking back. Claire sighed.

Was anyone else coming? Cars were jammed nose to tail along the narrow road, some double parked, and multiple For Sale signs were poking out of walls, windows and doorways, but she couldn't see any people. She looked at her watch. It was nearly four o'clock. Open viewing was almost over, but it was too early for a glass of wine. She groaned and wandered back to the kitchen to flip on the kettle.

Her mobile began to buzz on the table. She picked it up and saw it was a withheld number. 'Hello?'

'Dr Sharp, it's Peter. We met the other day at the National Gallery?'

'Oh, yes. Hello, Peter.'

'We were wondering if you'd had a chance to consider our proposal.'

Claire felt beads of sweat form at the back of her neck. 'Um, well, to be honest, Peter, it's an interesting case, but sadly it's a no.'

There was a pause.

'I'm sorry to hear that, Dr Sharp. And very disappointed,' Peter said at last.

There was another awkwardly long pause. Claire clenched her eyes shut. Why did this make her feel quite so uncomfortable? she wondered. There was something about Peter's manner that made her squirm, particularly as she now knew he was not much older than one of her students.

'Might there be room for negotiation, I wonder?' Peter said at last.

'I don't think so.'

'What if we were to offer you thirty thousand?' said Peter.

'What?' she gasped. Her heart punched hard in her chest. 'Peter, that's an awful lot of money.' She paused. 'Is it really worth that? I mean, for me it's not even about the money, really, it's about—'

'Look, Dr Sharp. If you're concerned about the ethics of what we are asking you to do, I can assure you that we are only interested in the truth. I'm sure you can appreciate that. And at the end of the day, we are simply offering to pay you for your professional services. There's no lie in this. Only truth.'

Claire glanced at the pile of bills stacked up on the kitchen counter. Correspondence from her lawyer itemising conveyancing charges lay open. She pushed her hand through her hair.

'I hear what you're saying, Peter, but my job is on the line here.'

'Not at all, Dr Sharp. Quite the contrary. You will be *doing* your job by unearthing the truth. Forgive me, Dr Sharp, but you are an art historian, are you not? Of some eminence. To allow history to be overlooked or simply rewritten to use an image for the purposes of marketing and politics is fraud. That needs to be corrected or we are all accepting a lie as part of our country's narrative.'

Claire was silent. She couldn't deny that Peter was extremely persuasive. Everything he had just said was true.

'Okay, I'll think about it,' she heard herself say. 'But—'

'Excellent news! I'll let you crack on, Dr Sharp. I'll be in touch very soon.' There was a click as he hung up.

The intercom buzzed, making Claire jump. She lurched into the hallway, her legs shaking, and snatched up the handset. She really couldn't face any more viewers. 'Hello?'

'Hiya, it's me.'

'Thank God, Jen.' Claire pressed the button to release the door. She then opened the front door and walked back through into the kitchen, chewing her thumbnail.

'How did the viewings go?' said Jen, now in the hall. 'Any potentials?' Claire heard the door shut and Jen came into the kitchen carrying a shopping bag. 'Everything okay? I thought you might like some vino and a few crisps.' She began to unpack the bag on to the kitchen counter. 'I also thought I'd treat us to some guacamole.' She was just about to take a couple of glasses out of the cupboard when she stopped and stared at Claire, who was still gnawing her thumbnail. 'You look white as a sheet,' she said. 'What's up?'

Claire sat down heavily on the window seat. 'I just took a call from Peter.'

'And?'

'And he raised the stakes. So I've done something, Jen.'

'Tell me.'

'I've said I'll think about taking a bribe of thirty thousand pounds,' said Claire, 'to lie about the creator of the most famous painting in Scotland.'

Jen raised her eyebrows and sucked air through her teeth. Then she grabbed two glasses from the cupboard and began pouring out the wine.

'Say something, Jen.'

Jen walked over to the window seat and handed Claire a glass. 'Well, if we're going to be up to our necks in organised crime, I wish I'd bought some salsa too,' she said, and took a large gulp of wine.

Chapter 9

18th century, Edinburgh

'Let this be the first real step,' said Katherine.
She and Francis Pringle were standing outside the theatre on Princes Street. Pringle was mustering up the courage to take his first walk in his new persona, and Foote and Smellie were there to see them on their way.

'Remember,' said Foote, 'bold and assertive, chin up, shoulders back and long, deep strides.'

Pringle smiled and nodded decisively, straightening his hat and adjusting his lapels.

'So.' He turned to Katherine. 'Just halfway down Princes Street and then back?'

'Yes,' she said. She patted his gloved hands. 'Don't

worry. I'll be with you at every step.'

'I am rather nervous, I must confess,' said Pringle. 'I fear everyone will point and stare. I'll be a laughing stock, and this little experiment will be over before it's even begun!'

'Nonsense,' said Foote. 'Commit to the character, my good man!' He winked.

Turning away from the encouraging faces of Foote and Smellie, Pringle somehow instinctively put out his arm to Katherine. She linked her hand through the crook of his elbow and off they went, the thespians, like over-protective parents, watching Pringle's every step, willing him on.

At first he felt his strides were stilted and wooden, until he realised that no one was staring. In fact, no one so much as gave them more than a passing glance. Instead, they received nods and smiles and the odd 'good morning' as they made their way along the thoroughfare. The sky was blue, the air crisp and clear, and with the magnificent castle looking down on them it really was a most delightful autumn day to be parading through the New Town. Pringle found himself beginning to relax. His shoulders eased, and his stride became more natural and comfortable.

'I must say, I'm rather enjoying myself,' he said.

'I don't mean to alarm you,' said Katherine, 'but our neighbours the Smeaton twins are walking towards us. And oh, how they like a gossip.'

'Heavens, no!' remarked Pringle through gritted teeth.

'Fear not,' muttered Katherine, quickening her pace. 'Leave this to me.' Pringle could sense her excitement at the challenge. 'Good day, Miss Smeaton, Miss Smeaton.'

'Ah, good day to you, Miss Hume,' said one.

'Good day, Miss Hume,' said the other.

The sisters were considerably older than their neighbour, with wispy white ringlets drooping under their hats. Their arms were linked and they were wearing identical garishly checked dresses with neat jackets over the top. A fat pug at their feet wore a bonnet trimmed in the same tartan. It seemed grateful to stop walking, and sat neatly, its tongue lolling.

There was a slightly awkward pause, but then Katherine composed herself and announced, 'Allow me to present to you Mr Francis Pringle, my second cousin. He has just arrived in Edinburgh from the Borders.'

It was said so smoothly that Pringle didn't even flinch. He smiled and gave a small bow. 'Ladies,' he said, his voice a little croaky with nerves. Katherine gave his arm a squeeze. He coughed, regaining his composure. 'I am delighted to make your acquaintance.'

The Smeaton sisters both smiled broadly and seemed to peer at Pringle curiously. Or did they? Perhaps they looked at everyone like this, Pringle told himself.

'Well, Mr Pringle, welcome to Edinburgh,' said one.

'Are you residing here in the New Town?' said the other.

Pringle's mind began to swim. He hadn't thought that far ahead.

'He is to take my brother's flat in James Court for the duration of his visit,' Katherine interjected quickly.

Pringle nodded and smiled. His cheeks were beginning to ache. He tried to relax his mouth but then feared his face was contorting in a strange way.

'It suits his work to be in the older part of town,' continued Katherine.

'My work?' Pringle tried not to sound too enquiring.

'Mr Pringle is a writer,' Katherine went on. 'A great observer of people and the human condition. He is working on a collection of poetry at the moment, but he writes prose too.' Both Smeatons let out appreciative noises. 'And now we must press on, as we have an appointment. Good day.' Katherine smiled.

'Good day,' the Smeatons replied in unison. They nodded, and seemed to give Pringle more lingering glances before walking on.

'A writer?' said Pringle, not turning his head.

'Indeed,' said Katherine, also looking straight ahead. But then she stopped and looked at Pringle. 'And a very good one too.'

'Did you just think of this now?' said Pringle.

'No,' said Katherine defiantly. 'Because you are a writer. You have been a writer your entire life. But because you are a woman no one has ever given you that title. You have always been "the wife of", "the mother of". And I "the sister of".' She rolled her eyes. 'Is that all we are? And yet your poetry and prose have been considered to be of the highest quality amongst the men of our circle, the men who are all allowed, quite freely, to call themselves writer, philosopher, poet, doctor, scientist, historian . . . it is unjust. And so I say you, Francis Pringle, are a writer. And we shall see where your writing shall take you now! Embrace this great opportunity.' Katherine's cheeks were flushed, and her eyes were wide. She was a creature transformed, and Pringle nodded, processing the ideas that had sprung up in his mind at the words of his invigorated companion.

'And what about residing in your brother's flat?' he said. 'Shall I really live there?'

'Consider, my dear friend,' said Katherine. 'You can't very well carry on living in your own flat, can you? How on earth will you live as Francis Pringle if you keep changing back into Alison Cockburn every time you cross your threshold?' She shook her head. 'No, no, that will never do.'

Pringle wondered. Had he really thought he could just dress up as a man as and when it suited him? The transformation had taken a rather more consuming turn than perhaps he had considered it might. But Katherine was right. How could he be two people at once? And two genders? It would be . . . difficult. And, he realised, it wasn't unpleasant being Francis Pringle. He nodded at passing faces. Was it his imagination or was there the odd admiring glance from the ladies who smiled shyly in his direction? As a man, with Katherine's support, he might even try to have some of his writing published. What would have been unthinkable yesterday had suddenly become possible today.

'Katherine, my dear!' came a voice behind them.

They both turned to see David Hume climbing out of a carriage behind them. He was looking quite agitated. Katherine gave Pringle a squeeze of the arm.

'Now, my dear, for the greatest test so far!' she said with a confident smile. 'Convince my brother, and we shall be ready to introduce you to the literati!'

Chapter 10

Pringle could feel the heat of Hume's eyes on him. They were sitting in the drawing room of the Humes' New Town flat, awaiting the arrival of a number of guests for their annual St Andrew's Day soirée. Pringle had been practising a new way of sitting: legs apart, back poker straight, but leaning slightly forward. It felt peculiar. He had acquired some further garments from Mr Foote but had also been brave enough to visit a gentlemen's outfitter, where he had been measured for a fine wine-coloured coat, spending more money on clothes than he had ever done in his life. To wear a wig or not had been a question he had asked himself more than once, but he had decided that it was infinitely more comfortable to go wigless when it was acceptable to do so and instead simply brush his hair off his face and wear it clubbed at the nape of his neck with a ribbon. A powdered wig, he considered, might be appropriate for more formal gatherings. The eyeglasses Smellie had given him had been a stroke of genius, for despite their small size they felt almost like a mask, something to hide behind. He decided to wear them pushed forward on his nose and peer over them. This, he felt, gave him a somewhat intellectual air of wisdom and authority.

'You will draw attention to him if you keep staring like that, brother,' hissed Katherine.

'I can't help myself,' said Hume incredulously. 'I find it all rather astonishing, I have to admit.' Lowering his voice to a whisper, he continued, 'When I first saw you with him, yesterday morning, I was quite convinced of his being a complete stranger to me. And now, with him sitting not two feet away, I'm still unsure!'

He frowned and stared harder still.

'Oh, for pity's sake, Mr Hume!' said Pringle. 'You know me! You must adjust to my new appearance before the guests arrive, or you will reveal the disguise and our little experiment will be smashed to smithereens. We must hope that those who know me as Alison don't recognise me.'

'In no time at all,' Hume blethered on, ignoring Pringle, 'you have become somebody completely new! Moving into my flat, no less! The wheels of this "experiment" as you call it are spinning so quickly that I haven't had a chance to catch up. It's rendered me quite speechless.'

'Well, it does not sound like it,' snapped Katherine.

'But consider, my dears, you are asking me to lie!' said Hume. 'Lie to my good friends! To Mr Smith, the dearest and best of men! My closest confidant!'

Katherine threw up her hands. 'Not lie, brother. 'Tis just a wee jest!'

'Pray, Mr Hume, don't take it too seriously,' said Pringle. 'See it as "social analysis". Observe in your own brilliant way, and then it will provide you with much to think and indeed write about.'

Hume rubbed his chin 'I'm not sure.'

Katherine groaned.

They were interrupted by a sharp knock on the front door.

'Brother!' snapped Katherine. 'You must compose yourself, and quickly!'

Hume and Pringle stood as the door opened and the housekeeper, Peggy, bobbed a curtsey. 'Madam, sir,' she said, 'Mr Adam Smith and Mr Allan Ramsay.'

'Ah, my dear fellows,' said Hume, pumping their hands in turn. 'Do please be seated.' He waved his hands in the direction of the many elegant chairs that were scattered around the room, but the visitors stood quite still. There was a moment of awkwardness.

'Brother,' said Katherine with a tinkly laugh, 'you have forgotten to introduce our dear cousin, whom our guests have never set eyes on before.'

'Oh, yes,' bumbled Hume. 'My cousin . . . my cousin! Of course, my cousin.'

There was a pause.

'Who is?' Katherine prodded between gritted teeth.

'Ah, yes. Mr Smith, Mr Ramsay, allow me to present my second cousin, Mr Prancis Fingle.'

'Pringle,' Pringle corrected. 'Francis Pringle.'

Katherine rolled her eyes as Hume blushed. 'Of course, Pringle,' he muttered. 'Pringle. Mr Francis Pringle.'

Smith and Ramsay appeared surprised but bowed politely, and Pringle gave a small bow to each gentleman. 'Mr Smith and Mr Ramsay, delighted,' he said.

A flustered Hume didn't seem to know whether to stand or sit.

Peggy came back into the room with a tray of glasses filled with claret, and the awkwardness of the moment was broken. Hume seized a glass and took a large gulp.

'Second cousin to the Humes?' said Smith, easing himself into a chair. 'And I thought I knew everything there was to know about my dearest friend. What brings you to Edinburgh?'

'Yes,' said Hume. 'What *does* bring you to Edinburgh . . . cousin?'

Pringle was aware of Katherine sucking in her cheeks.

He felt a trickle of sweat run down his neck and hoped very much that the flush he was sure was visible would be attributed to the flames that raged in the fireplace.

'I am hoping that your fair city might serve as muse to my writing,' he said. 'For, you see, I am a writer of poetry. And some prose too. I like to study people and their lives. The humdrum, the everyday, the beauty in simplicity.' At this, Smith and Ramsay seemed to nod and smile approvingly. 'And to my mind there is no finer city than Edinburgh in which to observe life in all its rather glorious chaos,' Pringle added. This was met with murmurs of agreement.

'Ah, so you have visited before?' said Ramsay.

Before Pringle had to answer this, there was another knock on the door, and everyone but Katherine stood as more visitors were ushered in.

'Mr Robert Burns and Mr Adam Ferguson,' said the housekeeper.

And as attention was diverted to the latest guests, Pringle took a moment to remember to breathe before greeting the new arrivals. He looked over to Katherine, who gave him an encouraging smile and the tiniest of winks.

'A fellow poet for you to meet, Pringle,' said Hume, smiling. 'Perhaps our very own "heaven-taught plough-man", Mr Burns here, might like to read some of your verses?' Pringle smiled politely, his eye twitching somewhat, and he noticed a slight snarl on the lips of Katherine. She seemed set to slap her brother with the fan she held gripped in her fist.

'Any ladies joining us tonight?' said Burns, glancing around the room with a twinkle in his eye. Fortunately for Pringle, tonight he was more interested in the fairer sex than in a stranger's poetry.

'I'm a wench and not a lady?' Katherine pouted.

'Ah, Miss Hume, forgive me,' said Burns, reaching out to kiss her hand. 'There is no finer and bonnier a hostess than your good self, other than perhaps Mrs Alison Cockburn. Will she be joining us? I do so enjoy Mrs Cockburn's company.'

Pringle sensed Hume's panic without daring to look at him. Instead, he kept his eyes firmly fixed on Katherine, who, without so much as a flicker of hesitation, announced, 'Ah, Mr Burns, our dear Mrs Cockburn has gone to Glasgow to visit her son. But our friend Mrs Agnes McElhose, whom I don't believe you have met, is due to join us.'

Once again there was a knock on the door, and it opened to admit two further guests, the demure Mrs McElhose, whom everyone called Nancy, and the delightfully familiar Mr Samuel Foote, who acted his role of stranger to Pringle smoothly and with exquisite charm.

'Our little party is complete,' announced Hume, seeming more relaxed now. 'And so let us make our way to the dining room, where we can sup and converse, and be merry on this St Andrew's night!'

'I am rather surprised,' said Pringle, 'that you are marking the day of one of the apostles, given your scepticism regarding the church, dear cousin.'

There was a roar of laughter.

'You should know by now, my good man,' said Hume with a chuckle, 'that my "faith" is never shaken where there is a feast to be had! Come, dear friends, let us eat!'

And without thinking, he patted Pringle's shoulder as they walked into the dining room.

Chapter 11

21st century, Drumlanrig Castle

'Right,' said Jen. 'We've got about an hour and a half so let's get all the facts straightened out.'

'Can you drive and think at the same time?' said Claire.

'Multi-tasking, you mean?' said Jen. 'Never been my strong point. So for God's sake keep it simple. My addled brain can't handle too much complication.'

They were heading out of Edinburgh in Jen's car, driving south-west towards Dumfries and Galloway and the grandeur of Drumlanrig Castle.

'Right, there're two strands to this,' Claire began. 'First of all, we prove it's *not* a Raeburn – by throwing doubt on the pose, the style and the likelihood that he painted this actual picture. Concrete evidence would be good here. That's the bit we give to Peter.'

'Yes, that I understand,' said Jen, nodding. 'And it's not signed, is it? So that helps.'

'Correct,' said Claire. 'But Raeburn rarely signed his work. And *then* we prove it's the work of someone else, namely Danloux.'

'But, my dear, you said you don't think it is by Danloux.'

'We have to take what I think out of the equation,' said Claire. 'I have to approach this like a lawyer representing a criminal. I might in my gut believe the criminal is guilty, but I can gather enough evidence to prove otherwise.'

'You mean tell porkies?'

Claire looked sheepish. 'Not porkies as such, just strong, conclusive evidence.'

'So why Drumlanrig? And more importantly, do they have a tea room?'

'Three reasons. Well, actually, four,' Claire told her. 'One, they have a couple of Raeburns I'd be interested in seeing; two, they have I think five Danloux paintings that it would be very helpful to examine close up; three, the curator is a friend of mine – Eleanor Strange – and I think she might have some insights; four, frankly, I just need to get out of Edinburgh for the day. A change of scenery might help to clear my head.'

'And the tea room?'

'One of the best,' said Claire. 'All the finest Scottish delicacies: scones, empire biscuits, toasties, lentil soup! Lunch is on me.'

'Right, I have an incentive,' said Jen. 'Okay, run past me all the reasons our skating minister is *not* a Raeburn, then. And remember, I'm not an art historian, so none of your big words.'

'Well, think of the Raeburn Room at the university. The room has six portraits that are typical of his style.'

'Musty is the word that comes to mind for me,' said Jen. 'Posed, quite dark and gloomy, dramatic lighting, rather traditional, bourgeois. Wouldn't look out of place in a gentlemen's club or stately home.'

'Exactly. Now consider the Skating Minister.'

'It's completely different. Mainly because the subject is moving, but also he's in profile rather than face on. The colours are quite different too, not dark and depressing, and of course it's outside. I would also say – how very daring of me – that it's sort of . . . *fun*? Whimsical, even? There's a little bit of joy and affection in that painting.'

Claire nodded. 'In short, it just doesn't fit,' she said, staring out at the countryside. 'Remember, Raeburn mainly painted indoors. In a studio – a "practice", if you will. This painting would have been tricky to do indoors as he needed to capture the physicality of the skater. That's not a pose you can keep up other than actually in the act of skating. Think of the balance. The way the skater leans in order to propel himself forward. I mean, you can't balance in that pose, can you?'

'Not without ropes. So maybe he just did preliminary sketches outside and then finished it off in the studio?' Jen suggested.

'Possibly,' said Claire. 'But that wasn't really his thing. He was a portrait painter – that was his job. It was how he made his money. Would this really have been the portrait that the Reverend Robert Walker wanted or expected? Chew on that one.'

As they finally arrived at Drumlanrig, Jen sighed. 'My brain's hurting.'

'Maybe you just need a coffee?'

'And a pee. I'll come and find you. Just carry on without me.' She set off in search of the toilets.

Claire took in her surroundings. The castle was quite magnificent, like a children's drawing, with turrets and flags. The seat of the Duke of Buccleuch for centuries, it was known as the 'pink palace' for good reason, with its red sandstone that glowed in the sunlight. She walked up the steps, and as she approached the door a tall, elegant woman appeared.

'This is an honour, Dr Sharp!' she said. 'Always a pleasure to have a visit from such an eminent art historian.'

Claire felt a stab of guilt. 'Well, good morning, Eleanor. It's very kind of you to see us.'

'Us?' Eleanor looked confused.

'My friend Jen has gone to the powder room,' said Claire. 'She's going to catch us up.'

Eleanor ushered Claire through the grand front door. 'So, Raeburn and Danloux paintings?' she said. 'This wouldn't have anything to do with our friend the Skating Minister, would it?'

Claire laughed nervously. 'I'm just doing some personal research.'

Eleanor looked sceptical. 'Claire Sharp, what are you up to?'

'Oh, nothing mysterious,' Claire said as lightly as she could. 'To be honest I'm working on a proposal for a book on Raeburn. You know it's something I've always wanted to do. Something accessible, not too academic. For the commercial market. And the mystery surrounding the Skating Minister is always going to be of interest.'

Eleanor nodded. 'Absolutely. It's compelling. Well, shall we press on?' She waved Claire past the ticket desk, telling them to look out for Jen, and led the way inside. 'So, assuming we're disproving Raeburn as the artist, shall we begin with Danloux?'

'Perfect,' said Claire.

They set off through the vast corridors and then up a grand staircase. The rooms were opulent, with high ceilings and dark wood panelling, yet the castle felt homely. Claire found herself walking faster than was comfortable to keep up with Eleanor, who had set off at a brisk clip. Keys hanging on a chain from her waist swung and jangled as she moved. Everywhere Claire looked were extraordinary works of art adorning the walls like casually hung baubles: curiosities to brighten dark corners. A Rembrandt here, a Gainsborough there. Monarchs from all periods, trussed up in silks and ruffs, stared down from elaborate frames.

'I know I say it every time I come here, Eleanor, but this collection is staggering,' said Claire.

'It's more than a little impressive,' Eleanor agreed. 'Stuffed to the gunnels, we are. And still acquisitions are made, rooms are reorganised, paintings are moved to new locations. Nothing stands still. It well and truly keeps me on my toes.'

Finally, they entered a starker, simpler hallway. It was an armoury, hung with broadswords and rifles. The paintings that covered the walls here were devoted to the military.

'Well, here are two of the key paintings to support the case for Danloux, as it were,' said Eleanor.

Claire gazed at the two pictures, which were placed on either side of a doorway. Both were of soldiers wearing traditional military red. In one portrait, the soldier was running towards the viewer, his left leg stretched behind him in an almost balletic pose, a spear clasped in his hands as if to be launched at any second. His face was that of a petulant boy, staring with cold emotion.

In the second, the soldier was poised to fire a musket, his shoulders raised, his legs wide, his face deep in concentration. Although his finger wasn't on the trigger, it was stretched in anticipation, the red cloth of his waistband flowing in the breeze.

'The master of the action shot,' Claire mused.

'Nice legs too,' said Jen, coming in to join them. She was a little out of breath and had to mop her brow with a tissue from her pocket.

'Eleanor, let me introduce my good friend and colleague, Professor Jennifer Brodie,' said Claire.

Eleanor smiled and reached out to shake Jen's hand. 'I agree, professor, he does have a shapely calf. Much like our skating minister, wouldn't you say?'

'Not sure that's enough to prove Danloux was the artist,' said Claire.

'No, perhaps not, but there's definitely real energy in this painting. Much like the minister,' said Eleanor. 'Raeburn's work always strikes me as characterful but static. And the scale of the figures here, by Danloux, is similar to the Skating Minister, which is very small in comparison to other Raeburns.'

'I'm still doubtful that Danloux painted the

minister,' said Claire. 'It just doesn't add up. He took commissions from aristocrats – for example, your Duke of Buccleuch. So why paint a random clergyman in Edinburgh skating on a frozen loch?'

'What do you think, Eleanor?' Jen asked.

Eleanor smiled, and then shrugged. 'Was it painted by Danloux? There's a possibility, I suppose. You can . . .' she paused briefly, 'contrive an argument to suit it if you really put your mind to it. It's just words, after all. He happened to be in Edinburgh at the time; he was experimenting with new techniques and so forth. Personally, I've never believed it was Raeburn, so it's certainly interesting to speculate that it might have been Danloux. But you'll never convince the powers that be in the National Gallery unequivocally of that until you find the missing painting.'

'Oh,' said Jen, her eyes widening. 'There's a missing one?'

'Yes, I hadn't quite filled you in on all the details yet, Jen,' said Claire. 'I thought we'd build up to that.'

Chapter 12

'Listed in an Edinburgh auction house called Dowell's, in George Street,' Claire began, 'in 1896 I think it was, there was a Raeburn painting labelled as *The Late Dr Walker*. That's our minister,' she added.

'Purchased anonymously,' Eleanor interjected. 'And now considered "missing".'

Claire nodded. They were strolling in the grounds of the castle, having descended from the elegant gravel terrace down wide, sweeping stairs to lawns surrounded by decorative, sculpted hedges. Various levels and gentle slopes lay before them, and forest-covered hills rolled away into the distance. The castle itself loomed behind them.

'This missing painting is believed to be in the form of one of those "musty" portraits you described earlier,' she told Jen. 'A traditional pose of a clergyman dressed in black.'

'In fact, Raeburn painted one of his colleagues from the Canongate kirk in the same style,' said Eleanor. 'So we assume it's very similar in its form.'

'A plea was put out some years ago now for owners of private collections to scour their portraits to see if it could be located,' Claire went on, 'but to no avail. Mind you, it was mainly advertised in Scotland.'

'It could be that it was miscatalogued or labelled incorrectly at some point in its sale history,' said Eleanor.

Jen frowned. 'But, if you don't mind my ignorance, so what? I mean, what difference does it make? Missing or not, how does this affect the provenance of our skating minister, the one in the National Gallery?'

'If this missing portrait could be found, it would add a lot of weight to the argument that the Skating Minister is *not* a second portrait of Walker by Sir Henry Raeburn, given that it's not his style, et cetera et cetera.'

Jen nodded. 'Ah, I see. So where might this missing one, the supposed "real" one, have gone?'

Eleanor shrugged. 'No idea. But the fact that it was well documented in the papers, in a documentary on the BBC and in art periodicals that it was "out there", and yet no one has come forward to declare they have it, implies it's vanished from circulation.'

'Disappearing out of circulation means what exactly?' asked Jen.

'It might have been destroyed in a fire, or lost, or stolen,' said Claire. 'Maybe it's languishing in someone's attic or garage.'

'These things can emerge quite surprisingly and randomly in sale rooms. Essentially when people need cash. They are rarely "found",' Eleanor added. 'I think you should give up on that, really.'

Jen scratched her chin. 'Okay, I think I follow, but when it was sold, back in, when was it, 1896, who might the anonymous buyer have been? I mean, look at it this way, *who* would have wanted to purchase a musty old portrait of a clergyman? It's hardly something you'd want to hang in your living room, is it? And the portrait you're describing doesn't sound like a thing of beauty. So a collector of Raeburns must have bought it, no? In which case it must be out there in someone's collection, mustn't it?'

'Could be, but again, it would be strange if a collector with a good knowledge of the art world wasn't aware of the current controversy,' said Claire.

'So, then, it could have been purchased by someone with a connection to Walker? For sentimental reasons?'

'Well, it was actually sold by one of the Walker family, so that's not particularly likely,' said Eleanor.

'Okay, fair enough. But he was a minister, so the connection could have been to do with his work?' Jen went on. 'Ministers were very highly regarded back then; there was real affection for them. They were pillars of the community.'

'Well, he was based at the kirk in Cramond for part of his career before moving into the city centre, was he not?' said Claire. 'That would mean it was somewhere fairly local.'

'The other aspect of the Reverend Robert Walker's life that's not really widely known is that he was an abolitionist,' said Eleanor. 'I remember reading that in Ghana, at one of the monstrous slavery castles on the coast, there is mention of Walker – honouring him for the part he played in bringing about the abolition of slavery.'

Claire frowned. 'I didn't know that,' she said, stopping to turn and look at Eleanor.

'Oh, yes. I wouldn't be surprised if the painting was purchased by someone who then gifted it to a museum in Ghana, or another African country,' said Eleanor. 'It's probably in a glass case somewhere.'

'Raeburn, though, had links to the slave trade.' Claire's mind began to race as she attempted to recall information. 'He was appointed to oversee the sale of a Jamaican plantation, including the sale of slaves.'

'And many of those "respectable gentlemen" he painted, and was commissioned and paid by, were also supporters and profiteers of the slave trade. You could say Raeburn himself profited from it directly.'

'But it has always been documented that Raeburn and Walker were great friends.' Claire muttered this more to herself.

'Friends can still have opposing viewpoints, I suppose,' said Jen.

'Oh, this was more than just an opposing idea,' said Eleanor. 'Robert Walker was bitterly opposed to slavery. He persuaded the presbytery of Edinburgh to petition for the ending of the slave trade. He was rather more influential than just a skater.'

'So based on this information,' said Claire, 'it seems highly unlikely that Walker and Raeburn had quite such a lovely bond as previously thought.'

'Professional respect, yes; they were both members of the prestigious Royal Company of Archers,' said Eleanor. 'And remember, Raeburn was one of the trustees of Walker's will. So there was undoubtedly a high level of regard there. But a warm, convivial friendship?' She shrugged. 'Hard to imagine.'

'There's something else,' said Claire. 'The question of why paint the skating picture in the first place. Raeburn was a jobbing portrait painter. He did it for the money, pure and simple. So why paint Walker skating at all? If, as we suspect, he painted him in a traditional portrait form, it wasn't an act of friendship. It was a job. He'd have received payment for it.'

'So the painting of the minister skating was what,

then?' Jen asked. 'Doesn't make sense he would paint it as a gift if they weren't great chums.'

'Exactly,' said Claire. 'A serious, well-respected clergyman wouldn't have commissioned a portrait like that, and given that it's actually unlikely they *were* great friends nor would Raeburn have done it as a freebie.'

Eleanor's phone began to ring. She looked at the screen. 'Sorry, I have to get this. Look, I'll leave you here if that's okay. I really ought to get back to work. It's been . . . illuminating, as ever, Dr Sharp,' she said with a wry smile, beginning to walk away towards the castle.

'Thank you so much, Eleanor,' Claire called after her.

'Keep me posted,' Eleanor replied, 'you're definitely on to something. Not sure what, though!'

Chapter 13

18th century, Edinburgh

rancis Pringle awoke with a crusty mouth, the most desperate drouth and a thumping headache. He stumbled out of bed and fumbled around in the dark, frigid room for the jug of water he knew was sitting on his nightstand. Something crashed to the floor, but finally he laid his hands on the cold surface of the jug and lifted it directly to his lips without trying to locate a cup. But nothing happened. He realised that the surface was frozen and plunged a fist through the ice, feeling the freezing water on his fingers. Then he tried to drink again, allowing lumps of ice to rest on his nose as the water underneath gushed into his mouth. He gulped as though it were life-giving, allowing it to dribble down his chin and soak the top of his nightshirt. But when he reached with his left hand to feel the damp garment he realised he wasn't actually wearing a nightshirt. In fact, he was still fully dressed, complete with coat. As he put a hand up to his head, he felt a hat too, and by some miracle his eyeglasses were still clamped to his nose.

He put the jug down on the floor and sat on the edge of the bed, removing his hat to rub his forehead. Not only was his head fit to explode, his stomach was lurching rather alarmingly. And with little warning other than a growing unease that something was brewing down below, he grabbed the chamber pot from under the bed and promptly threw up.

Not since he had eaten a nasty Nor' Loch eel pie in his youth had he felt quite so out of sorts. He lay back on the pillow, clutching the cloth from the nightstand to his mouth, helpless to do much more. The room was now spinning and he squeezed his eyes shut, but this offered no respite, as events from the previous evening began to flood over him with rising uneasiness, from mild anxiety to toe-curling embarrassment.

Where exactly, he reflected, had it all gone awry? He began the tortuous process of piecing together the events of the evening.

Had it been during the soup course, as they had supped on steaming bowls of smoky Cullen skink?

It had been quite delicious: that was a fragment of memory that he didn't mind. The entire meal in fact had been a feast of delights. Yes, it was over the Cullen skink that someone . . . possibly Burns? No, not Burns. He had been too engrossed in talking to Nancy. It must have been Smith who had remarked that it was the perfect dish for a cold night. At that point someone else, perhaps Ramsay, had stated that there would be a hard frost that night – hard enough for the lochs to become skating rinks once more. As the conversation progressed, Hume had become quite excited. Pringle remembered through the flicker of the candles that Hume's wig was sliding a little off centre, his face was glowing with beads of sweat, a small dribble of gravy (from the excellent mutton collops) had settled on his chin, and he was clearly bursting to say something. Suddenly, he announced that Pringle was keen to join the Edinburgh Skating Club. Pleased with the impression he had created, he continued to talk, the momentum and the claret carrying him along with the storytelling. Pringle had frozen; Katherine was desperately trying to catch her brother's eye to warn him not to say any more. But Hume went on to inform the whole table that his second cousin was in fact a keen ice skater, having learned the skill during a spell in Amsterdam. Pringle groaned audibly at the memory. Amsterdam, of all places, where skating was commonplace and accomplished. Pringle had never skated in his life, although he had skited many times on wet dung, on the High Street, before landing on his backside.

Hume had continued, stating proudly (good God, from where on earth did this pride emanate? Pringle thought now) that Pringle would be a most excellent addition to the club. In fact, he pronounced, waving his fork in the air, his cousin would, with his athleticism and vigour, put all the other members to shame. Pringle had never witnessed such passion from Hume before.

At that point – Pringle remembered that it was as they had been eating an exquisite flummery – Katherine had attempted to smooth over this nightmare moment. She suggested that her brother was prone to gross exaggeration through the generosity of his spirit, and that Pringle would no doubt be a little rusty as it had been many years since his very brief stay in Amsterdam. But then Foote had made matters worse by contradicting her. Why, for heaven's sake, did he do that? Pringle threw up his hands to the ceiling, protesting to the darkness of his bedchamber as he remembered Foote saying that once you learned to skate it stayed with you for life. *He* had learned as a boy in Cornwall, and then, when he lived in London, had taken to the ice to skate regularly with the London Skating Club. As a young man, he boasted, before he had lost his leg, he had been known as 'the angel of the ice' as his grace was thought to be quite ethereal.

As Foote had begun his ridiculously self-indulgent tale Pringle had attempted to kick him under the table. Unfortunately, as he was sitting to the actor's left, he could only reach his wooden leg, and so the insufferable man had continued.

'How I long to skate again,' he had moaned, peering morosely into his wine glass. 'To skate is to feel, to be at one with Mother Nature and her icy blast! But with one leg 'tis only a distant memory.' At this he had wiped a tear from his cheek, the drunken fool.

And then Hume had said, 'Tomorrow we shall skate, Foote! We, your dearest friends, shall help you back on to the ice! What do you say, Pringle? We shall all skate! I shall skate too! And everyone shall see that Pringle here must become a member of the Edinburgh Skating Club!' And everyone had cheered raucously, raising their glasses.

There must certainly have been something glacial about the smile on Pringle's face as he had reluctantly raised his glass. He consoled himself now with the thought that this most ridiculous declaration would surely be forgotten, lost in the drunken mist of the evening.

Did they then have cheese? Clutching his pulsating forehead, Pringle groaned. Yes, they had had cheese.

He remembered because it had been at this point that Pringle himself had made the calamitous mistake of standing up alongside Katherine and Nancy to leave the room when the port was brought in, causing at first awkwardness, and then riotous laughter. Burns had made some comment about 'a man's a man for a' that . . . until he's a woman', at which point Hume had nearly combusted with laughter.

And Foxey! Oh, heavens above, Foxey! If he had jumped on Pringle's knee once during the evening, he'd done it ten times. And when he wasn't trying to get on his knee, he was staring adoringly up at him by his chair. Clearly the rescue on the High Street had bonded them for life. And every time he sidled up to Pringle, Smith noticed, and said, repeatedly, 'That dog knows you, man! He is attending to you most loyally!'

He had seemed quite baffled, and the way in which he spoke of Foxey's behaviour was a combination of awe and something like envy. 'I have never known him to do that with men other than Hume,' he had declared. 'He normally doesn't like men at all – or visitors! I have known this dog since he was a pup and still he curls his lip at me. In fact, come to think of it, the only person I've seen him show a fondness for other than Hume and Katherine is Alison Cockburn!'

Pringle had swiftly shoved Foxey off his knee, whereupon. Foxey had yowled in shock and slunk away, throwing Pringle a look of hurt. Pringle had hoped that would be the end of it.

Staying with the men in the dining room and trying to compensate for his mortifying slip-up, with the blasted dog threatening to give away his disguise, *and* by way of just trying to keep up, Pringle had drunk over-much port and whisky and sung riotous songs, recited poetry, and laughed like a wheezing pig. Now, in strange and blurry flashbacks, he remembered Katherine's face, a mixture of concern and amusement in the flickering candlelight as Burns and Ramsay had half-carried him down to the street and put him in a carriage, where he had slithered to the floor and been thrown around like a rag doll as they'd ascended the High Street over the teeth-rattling cobbles.

Snow had been falling as he had fumbled and slipped his way along the icy close to the James Court apartment, and he had struggled for what seemed like hours to get his key in the door. Finally, he had fallen inside and crawled to his bed.

Pringle felt numb. Had he given away his disguise while intoxicated? Shame, fear, and the purest form of anxiety he had ever suffered, exhausted him so much that he drifted once more into sleep, and so did not hear a key entering the lock or the footsteps in the hallway.

Chapter 14

Pringle opened an eye. Someone was holding a lantern, looking down at him, and in the glowing light he saw the face of Katherine Hume, a fur-trimmed hat perched above it. Was this a dream? There was another face there too. It was Samuel Foote. Was this in fact a nightmare?

'Good morning!' said Katherine, grinning broadly. 'My dear man, you were snoring like a cow in profound distress.'

'I must say, he doesn't appear to be in the rudest of health,' said Foote, raising a disapproving eyebrow.

'Francis,' said Katherine, 'you need to get up and get dressed . . . although now I look at you I see that you never actually undressed.'

'What?' Francis managed to utter. 'What on earth are you doing here, Katherine? And why is Mr Foote here also?'

'We, my dear fellow,' said Foote, with the theatricality that was beginning to grate, 'are going to teach you how to skate!'

'Now?' Francis raised his head a little. 'No, no, no! This must be a bad dream.' He closed his eyes and put his hands over his face.

'When else can you learn? You don't want anyone to see that you've never done it before, do you?' said Katherine. 'Mr Foote is going to lend you his ice skates and we decided last night that the best time would be early morning, when no one else is around. There has been a hard frost and we are sure the lochs must be frozen.'

'But damn and blast!' wailed Francis. 'How early? It's still dark! What time is it? And how in God's name did you get in here?'

'I used to live here, remember?' said Katherine curtly, the amusement leaving her face. She bustled around the room looking for a candle to light. 'And do not curse so! This is still my brother's apartment, so of course we have a key. And it's around seven o'clock, which gives us a good hour to practise before sunrise. Come, come, Francis, look lively!'

'I think our dear friend over-imbibed last night, Katherine,' said Foote, wagging a gloved finger.

'How on earth are you up and about so bright and

cheerful before cockcrow, Foote?' snapped Francis. 'Does your head not pound too?'

Foote gave a cheerful wave of his hand. 'My head is gin clear, my dear man.'

Pringle groaned. 'I'm really not fit to walk, let alone skate.'

'We shall give you a moment,' said Katherine. 'Mr Foote and I will wait in the parlour.'

'When does your maid arrive?' asked Foote.

'I don't have one,' said Pringle. 'I can't risk anyone finding out the truth, remember.'

'Ah,' said Foote. 'Well then, we shall leave you to fill your pot. And do use the proper vessel for it.' At this Katherine lost her stiffness and began to chuckle.

'I'm afraid my sense of humour is rather deficient this morning,' said Pringle. 'What do you mean?'

'You don't remember what happened last night with the filling of the pot?' Katherine asked, her hand over her mouth.

'What?' snapped Pringle, covering his ears. 'Tell me, I beg of you. But quietly.'

'We'll leave you to your toilet,' said Katherine, 'and then we shall reveal all.' She and Foote giggled like schoolchildren as they left the room, shutting the door behind them. It was insufferable.

Francis sat up and groaned. He realised that he had no choice; Katherine could be quite insistent when she wanted to be. His head still throbbed, but the nausea had passed and he shuffled over to the nightstand for the jug of water, which he carried to his dressing table. He filled the bowl with what was left of the water and splashed his face, wincing at the icy shock. He glanced at himself in the looking glass and was horrified by the image that looked back at him. He was deathly white, and there were bulbous bags under his eyes. That, he told himself, was the first and last time he would attempt to drink with the same fervour as his dinner companions. How on earth could they consume so much?

He glanced down at the spew-filled chamber pot that lay reeking like a dirty secret. He took a deep breath, flipped up his coat tails, pulled down his breeches and hunkered over it. His thighs were aching and there was a tweak of pain in his back. Now the memory of having to relieve himself last night flashed into his mind. He closed his eyes and began to sweat. He knew what had been the cause of Katherine and Foote's sniggering.

With no ladies present, some of the male guests had simply peed at the table, passing round a chamber pot. He had held on until he had felt fit to burst, when even in his inebriated state he had managed to excuse himself from the dining room without drawing too much attention. As soon as he left the room, though, he found himself dancing around in the hallway, unable to think rationally. In desperation, he had grabbed the flowers out of a large vase on the hall table and taken the pot into the nearest room to relieve himself, crouching in such an uncomfortable manner that he had strained the muscles in his thighs and, it seemed now, in his back too.

'How did you know?' he said through the closed door to Katherine and Foote. 'About the vase. I don't remember telling anyone.'

Katherine called out, 'Because it was my room you sneaked into. Nancy had gone home, and I had fallen asleep on my bed. I woke up just as you were relieving yourself. I knew it was you because you were singing, if you can call it that, and as you left the room I followed you out.'

'Why didn't you say anything?'

'I did not wish to cause you any embarrassment, dear friend.'

'Until now?'

'But even if I had called out, you wouldn't have heard.'

'What, pray, did I do with the vase?' said Pringle, cringing in anticipation of the answer.

'You simply put it back on the table and stuffed the flowers back in.'

Pringle shook his head. 'Well, I hope that is all,' he said sheepishly. He opened the bedroom door and staggered out into the parlour to join them, rubbing his back from where the pain was emanating. 'I really don't wish to know another thing!'

'Well, the flowers have wilted somewhat this morning,' said Katherine, smiling, but Foote gave a sharp intake of breath as he saw Pringle clearly for the first time.

'Oh dear. Even by candlelight, you do look rather green around the gills.'

Pringle scowled and picked up his gloves, which had miraculously made it home, and attempted to put them on, but his fingers refused to go into the right holes.

'As we proceed in this little experiment,' he muttered, still struggling with the gloves, 'last night's debauchery taught me some very important lessons. First of all, why didn't you leave out some sort of chamber pot for me? And whilst I can match the wit and intelligence of any man, I am a complete failure at matching their consumption of alcohol. They almost finished me off.'

Katherine tried to keep a straight face as she adjusted Pringle's hat and brushed dust from his shoulders. 'My dearest friend,' she said, 'I must congratulate you.'

'How so?'

'Well, you've been a man but two days and yet already you have adopted peevish qualities; 'tis a masculine habit to place blame at the feet of everyone but himself. Forgive a mere woman for pointing out that nobody forced you to take so much wine, port or whisky. And you yourself could have predicted that what you put in had to come out – one way or another.'

Pringle let out a chuckle and shook his head. 'Indeed, you are right. I apologise,' he said. 'I certainly don't feel myself. From now on, I will restrict myself to two glasses of wine.'

'Let us put last night behind us and take you to the ice,' said Foote as they headed out of the apartment and down the stairs, 'where the crisp air will restore you, body and mind.' He opened the street door and a blast of freezing air swept in.

'Where exactly are we going?' Pringle asked as they headed down the front steps and back up the close to a waiting carriage.

'Saint Margaret's Loch,' said Katherine. 'Let us hope that we have it all to ourselves!'

Chapter 15

21st century, Drumlanrig Castle

Jen looked lost in thought as she stirred her soup.

'Not hungry?' asked Claire, taking a bite from her ham roll.

'I know I'm never one to delay eating,' said Jen. 'But my brain is like mush and I just want to get this straight in my head. If all the evidence is leading us towards the idea that the painting is not a Raeburn – and this seems pretty watertight given everything we've just discussed about the relationship between the two men – then who on earth was this Danloux? And what was a Frenchman doing in Edinburgh painting pictures of random Church of Scotland ministers?'

'Well, it's a good question,' said Claire with a smile.

'He emigrated to London to escape the Revolution, I believe, and came to Edinburgh to paint some members of the French royal family also in exile living in Holyroodhouse. There was no connection between Danloux and Walker, as far as I know, so why he'd be painting a random minister on the ice I have no idea. But because he had painted that fine action shot of the soldier Eleanor showed us, and the cracking of the paint on the surface matches, suggesting a similar use of oils . . . oh, and as you mentioned, all the men have shapely calves . . . a connection was forged and a case for reattributing the painting was made.'

'But he wasn't painting the common man for shits and giggles?' said Jen, pointing her soup spoon at Claire.

'Crucially, he wasn't painting the common man,' said Claire.

'He was working for money?'

'Of course. And what's more, he worked for the aristocracy. He wasn't out capturing everyday scenes on the banks of Duddingston Loch.'

'How are you going to push this, Claire?' Jen shook her head. 'Really? None of it makes sense. Even I can see that this minister wasn't created by a posho portrait painter.'

Claire grimaced. 'I'm beginning to think it's just impossible I got all caught up in the moment . . . and the temptation of the money for doing something that seemed relatively simple. It kind of seemed like a harmless lie. And we art historians sometimes lose sight of the context and get preoccupied with the technicalities of the actual painting.'

'Well, half of it isn't a lie,' said Jen.

'True. I could definitely do half of it. I can put together a strong argument for its not being a Raeburn, probably with written or archival evidence on everything that Eleanor Strange told us about. But the second half of the deal, the Danloux bit, is somewhat problematic. Peter did say he was anxious for the truth, though, so that's all I can give him.'

Her phone beeped, and she glanced down at it. 'Speak of the devil,' she said. 'It's a text from a withheld number, but it's from Peter. Listen. "Good afternoon, Dr Sharp. I need to press you for an answer, I'm afraid, so I will call tomorrow. My friend is keen to get this wrapped up as quickly as possible. I hope the trip to Drumlanrig was fruitful. Peter."'

'Why all the rush?' said Jen with a curled lip. 'It's been a couple of hundred years. It's all a bit dramatic, isn't it?' Then she looked closely at her friend. 'Claire? Is everything okay? You look a bit funny.'

'I didn't tell him I was coming here,' said Claire slowly.

There was a silence.

'What do you mean?' Jen placed her soup spoon down and dabbed her lips with the napkin.

Claire frowned. Her mind was racing as she tried to piece it altogether.

'I don't understand,' she said. 'I didn't tell anyone I was coming here apart from emailing Eleanor yesterday. I didn't even tell *you* until you picked me up this morning. I just said we were going to have a day out.' She had a sense of rising panic, and glanced around nervously. 'Is he here? Has he followed us here?' Sweat was forming on her top lip. 'What the hell is going on?'

The tea room was relatively quiet, with just two other tables occupied, both by elderly couples. No one was looking at them.

'Claire,' said Jen calmly. 'Claire, stop panicking. Remember the last time you thought he'd been stalking you and it turned out there was a perfectly reasonable explanation. Let's think this through. Are you sure you didn't mention it when you met him?'

'I'm positive,' said Claire, trying to keep her voice low. 'I hadn't even thought of coming here myself at that point.'

'Well, in that case, there are two possibilities,' said Jen calmly. 'Either he's a master of disguise and he's dressed as an old woman sipping tea and eating shortcake over there, or he's heard it on the grapevine through that Strange woman – because she's in the art world and she's an expert in British portrait painters of the eighteenth century. Also, we're in a castle where there are several Danloux pictures, so it was likely you would come here. I could go on.'

Claire looked at the phone in her hand in horror and then back at Jen. She placed it on the table as if it were toxic. Then she rubbed her hands through her hair and exhaled.

'You're right I'm being completely paranoid,' she said. 'There must be a completely rational explanation.' She put her hand on her heart. 'Wow. That was an intense minute.'

'I think maybe this is a sign,' said Jen, 'that this job isn't for you. Look at you – you're actually shaking. Your nerves are all over the place. It's just a bloody painting, for goodness' sake.' She shook her head despairingly.

'I know, I know,' Claire said. 'You are completely right.'

'Phone him now,' said Jen.

Claire nodded. She scrolled back through her phone for his original number, tapped the screen and then pressed it to her ear.

'Dead,' she said. 'And his new number is withheld. When he phones tomorrow, I'll tell him I'm out.'

'Good,' said Jen. 'No more of this silliness.'

Claire nodded, picked up the silver teapot and poured them both another cup of tea.

'I know I said no more of this silliness, but can I just ask one tiny wee thing before we leave this?' said Jen as she pushed out her chair and stood up. 'So, we've established that the skating minister isn't a Raeburn, and probably not a Danloux either, therefore we really don't know who painted it? I mean, really, not a scooby?'

Claire threw her hands to the heavens. 'Nope,' she said weakly. 'We really are right back to square one on that one. I rather hoped Eleanor might offer us some blinding inspiration, but no, it's an absolute mystery. I really will have to revisit all Raeburn's contemporaries, but no one springs to mind.'

Jen nodded. 'You did say that before.' She set off towards the display cases of cakes and then stopped, turned round and trotted back. 'For that matter,' she said, 'how do we know that the skater is the Reverend Robert Walker? It could be someone else entirely.'

Claire looked at Jen and frowned. 'Oh God,' she said, 'I hadn't thought of that.'

Chapter 16

18th century, Edinburgh

It wasn't a particularly long journey down the street to St Margaret's Loch, situated beyond the Palace of Holyrood, but because of the light snowfall that had now frozen solid it was treacherous and painfully slow. The driver of the carriage cursed and complained so bitterly that everyone became quite anxious.

At last, the party of three decided it would be quicker and certainly less worrisome to walk, and so at the foot of Salisbury Crags they clambered out and set off. Katherine carried a lantern to light their way, but the sky was clear and a full moon shone over them, lighting up the path ahead. Their breath puffed and dispersed in white clouds as they crunched their way through the smattering of icy snow.

Foote stopped for a moment, leaned on his stick and caught his breath.

'Are you all right, Mr Foote?' Pringle enquired.

'It is so cold it hurts to breathe. And walking in these conditions is not ideal when you have a wooden leg.'

'Nor if your head pounds from over-indulgence,' Pringle admitted ruefully.

'Let us not complain,' said Katherine, 'but relish this singular opportunity to see the beauty of our surroundings whilst the rest of the city slumbers.'

Pringle smiled despite the discomfort thumping through his entire body at his friend's boundless optimism.

When the loch finally revealed itself before them it was an impressive sight. The frozen surface glittered under the moon with such brilliance, it was as though a myraid of diamonds had been scattered over the ground.

Katherine stopped. 'Oh my, isn't this quite a sight,' she said.

'Here are my skates,' said Foote, pulling them out of a bag he wore across his body. Pringle leaned against the lowest branch of a nearby tree, took off the gloves he had finally managed to struggle into and accepted the offered footwear. Katherine held the lamp aloft so he could see clearly what he was holding. The curved wooden frames were polished smooth, the curling blades underneath surprisingly heavy and cold to the touch. The base of each blade wasn't sharp but flat, about the width of the nail on his little finger, which reassured him that balancing wouldn't be quite the gravity-defying challenge he had assumed it would be. Long leather straps were looped through special slots on the skates so they could be attached securely to his own boots, and then secured by tapes.

'Do make sure you pull the inkles as tight as they will go,' said Foote, who seemed oblivious of a large drip hanging from the end of his nose. 'The skates must feel as though they are part of you.' So Pringle pulled the red linen tapes as tightly as he could around each foot, and with Katherine and Foote's help tottered towards the edge of the loch.

'I do hope the ice is strong enough,' he said.

'Have no fear.' Foote thwacked the surface with a large stick he had found by the lochside, then threw it with some force down on to the ice. It slid predictably, coming to a slow standstill a few feet away.

'Oh, so it holds the weight of a stick! That's very helpful,' said Pringle with a snort. 'Come on then, let's have a go. You'll have to pull me out if I go under.'

'Wait,' said Katherine. On tiptoes, she reached up and removed Pringle's spectacles. 'You really don't need these, and I fear they may not survive a fall. I don't much like the look of them anyway.' She slipped them into her pocket.

Pringle sighed. 'What an uplifting thought. You expect me to fall flat on my face. Well, wish me luck.'

Holding on to Katherine, he put one foot gingerly on the ice and then brought the other foot to join the first one, standing in a strange, hunched pose. His ankles wobbled.

'I shall step out a little way with you,' said Katherine, passing the lantern to Foote and holding on to Pringle as he began to move in an odd shuffling fashion.

'I shall stay here,' said Foote, 'in the wings, as it were. The moon shall be your illumination.'

He was right. The moon did cast a most pleasing glow, so that when Pringle looked down it appeared as though hundreds of candles were lit under the ice. As each leg moved he had to adjust his balance. It was the most peculiar sensation, especially since he still felt quite sick from the night before.

'Carefully does it,' said Katherine as they crept forward again.

'Try to straighten your body,' Foote encouraged from the lochside. 'At the moment, your behind is sticking out rather.'

'I'm preparing it for a sharp impact, so think of it as my cushion. Indeed I wish I had a real cushion tied round my waist,' said Pringle, easing forward again.

'I feel like a newborn lamb finding his feet for the first time.'

After a while, he progressed from shuffling to taking tiny steps, and Katherine began to move back a little. 'You've got it, Francis!' she exclaimed, just as he tried to straighten himself and lost his balance. Unable to right himself, hands flailing in every direction, he grabbed hold of Katherine and they both fell with a thud on to the ice.

'I fear you spoke too soon, my dear!' he said.

'Well, I'm not the slight wee creature I was in my youth, so at least we can be reassured that the ice is strong enough for you, given that we didn't fall straight through.'

'Get up, get up! Don't linger! Go again!' said Foote with a sweep of his arm. 'Don't fear the ice!'

Pringle staggered to rise and took Katherine's hand to help her up too. But then, predictably, just as Katherine had raised herself almost to standing, Pringle's balance began to waver. He veered backwards, then forwards, then backwards again, until finally he fell, his hat rolling off as he landed on his back with Katherine on top of him. Their laughter echoed around the crisp landscape, Foote hooting so loudly he could barely breathe.

'Never in all my days have I seen anything so comical as the two of you on ice!' he said.

'Katherine,' said Pringle, attempting to calm himself, 'I shall try to do this on my own, if you don't mind.'

He turned on to all fours and raised himself from squatting to standing, arms held wide. Tentatively, he pushed forward with one foot and then the other, and gradually the shuffle became longer sliding actions. It took many more falls and a lot more cursing before at last, after much encouragement from the lochside, Pringle found he was actually skating. 'I think I'm beginning to master this,' he said.

'Do try not to stick your tongue out as you skate,' said Katherine. 'It rather spoils the effect.'

'I'm concentrating so hard my face hurts. I expect it will be fixed for ever with a scowl and a protruding tongue!'

As Pringle became more confident, he began to look down less and was increasingly aware of the sensation of skating. He straightened up and momentarily closed his eyes. The freezing air blew across his face and through his hair and seemed to whip away the aches, pains and anxieties of the previous night. He picked up speed and took braver strides. He had never felt like this before, so out of control but somehow in control at the same time. Yet he was fully aware that all could be lost at any moment. It was by far the most exhilarating thing he had ever done.

He looked around and realised that the sun was

slowly rising. The sky was streaked pink, the trees silhouetted against the growing light and the long grasses stood white and crystallised at the edge of the loch, whose pristine surface was now marked with streaks and curves from his blades.

''Tis good to be back on the ice, is it not?' said a voice that Pringle did not recognise. He looked over to see a man on the bank of the loch putting on a pair of skates. The newcomer joined Pringle, skating effortlessly over to meet him.

'Good morning,' said Pringle. 'I am Francis Pringle, and it is a pleasure to meet you.'

'Indeed, indeed,' said the man, reaching out to shake his hand. He was of a similar height, and wore his grey hair tied back in a style that mirrored Pringle's own, but his handshake was so firm that it knocked his new acquaintance off balance.

'Oh, good Lord, Pringle,' said the man. 'Forgive me. Here I've almost knocked you over and I haven't even introduced myself yet.' He helped Pringle right himself. 'I'm Walker,' he said with a broad smile. 'The Reverend Robert Walker.'

Chapter 17

'**B**y Jove!' Foote declared as Walker and Pringle stood side by side on the ice. 'You could be brothers!'

It was true. Pringle could see, even in the pale dawn light, the physical similarities. They were the same height, and both had a strong jawline. But when it came to skating, the likeness ended. As Pringle perched on a tree stump to remove his skates, they discussed his interest in joining the Edinburgh Skating Club and Walker explained that, in order to be admitted as a member, he would have to demonstrate a few 'piffling' skills in front of the entire club at Duddingston Loch. Then a decision would be reached by ballot.

Pringle had attempted to sound quite at ease with the entire arrangement. But the cold and his fatigue had made his voice sound a little strange as he said, with a wave of his hand and a croak in his throat, 'Ah, yes, of course. I should be able to manage that without too much trouble.'

'It won't be a challenge for him,' Foote had added. 'Pringle learned in Amsterdam.' For that comment, he had received an earful from Katherine that lasted for the entire journey back into town.

Before their departure, Walker had kindly demonstrated (it was easier, he had explained, if he just showed them) the requisite skills as Foote, Pringle and Katherine stood on the banks of the frozen loch, mouths open in awe, and in Pringle's case in horror. Pringle had felt a tinge of annoyance, envy even, but no one could deny that the man was a joy to watch.

Walker was a most delightfully elegant skater. He could glide with ease, effortlessly cutting figures of eight as though he were slipping through soft butter, his arms folded across his chest and not waving about in the need for balance. He had demonstrated all the actions Pringle would need to perform, with comments such as 'My dear man, for an experienced skater this won't be much trouble at all' or 'A simple jump, nothing too ostentatious', this being said as he leapt into the air and landed with aplomb. Foote had applauded excitedly as Katherine muttered under her breath, 'Oh, Francis, your charm alone won't get you into this club!'

And then Foote had added, sotto voce, 'Heaven help

you, Pringle! It's just as well Walker didn't arrive ten minutes earlier to see you slithering around on your backside.'

Pringle had kept a smile fixed on his face but let out a tiny groan through gritted teeth. 'Yes, yes,' he had called out to Walker, 'no trouble. No trouble at all. I just need to practise.' Then, when the clergyman's back was turned, he had glanced heavenward in despair.

Foote and Katherine had looked sideways at each other and rolled their eyes, but then Katherine had slipped her arm through Pringle's and patted his arm. She knew, she had said in a soothing voice, that he was not the sort of person to give up without a fight. However, there was, she conceded, much work to be done.

'You and Miss Hume must come for luncheon, to the manse in Cramond,' Walker had said amiably. 'We can take a walk by the river and discuss the joys of skating and other outdoor pursuits.'

'We'd be delighted,' Katherine had answered before Pringle had a chance to concoct an excuse.

Chapter 18

Some two weeks after their encounter with the Reverend Robert Walker, Pringle and Katherine took a carriage out to Cramond. They set off early so as to arrive in time for the morning service at the kirk.

'What ails you, Francis?' said Katherine irritably. 'Are your breeches too tight? You can't sit still.'

Pringle sighed. 'Unlike that of my beloved son, who as you know is a well-respected minister-in-training, my faith is somewhat weak and imperfect, shall we say.'

Katherine frowned. 'Yes, I know. We have discussed this often.'

'It is one thing to pretend to the gentlemen of Edinburgh, infiltrate their clubs and become one of them. This is a social experiment, after all, as well as something of a jape. But I do wonder about sitting in the kirk in this guise. If the Lord – if there is one – can see who I truly am, then I become something of a deceiver. Dare I say it, a sinner? And then there's taking lunch with the good Reverend and his family. I confess I feel ill at ease. This is more than a jest, is it not, Katherine?'

Katherine was quiet as the carriage rolled on, clipping stones and bumping through potholes. They both sat looking out as the smoke and dirt of the town gave way to open fields and countryside, and it was some time before she responded.

'On balance, Francis, would you say that at this point in your life you are happy?' she asked.

'As Pringle?'

Katherine nodded.

Pringle considered this as he stared out of the carriage. There were fields now in every direction, the grassy fronds, white with frost, stretching down towards the River Forth, with Fife in the distance. What did 'happy' mean? He thought about his current state. He was certainly tired. It wasn't just the physical toll, the aches and pains of learning how to skate, in pursuit of which he had been in intensive training for the past two weeks. Pringle's bones ached, and he could feel muscles that he hadn't known he possessed, yet burning deep within him was a fire he had never experienced before. The flames of ambition had been lit and he was full of steely determination. He must succeed at all costs! To what end he had not considered, but the most challenging aspect, and perhaps the most exhausting, was keeping up the masquerade he was perpetrating. Never letting the mask slip, and seamlessly maintaining the persona of Francis Pringle, was mentally challenging enough. On top of this, like a snowball cascading down a mountainside gathering size and momentum, Francis had acquired new acquaintances every day since his transformation, and with them a burgeoning social scene. Everyone he met invited him here, there and everywhere. He had been well and truly burning the candle at both ends.

The outings had begun with a trip to the Theatre Royal with the Humes to see Mr Foote in all his magnificent splendour as Lady Pentweazel, and at supper afterwards they had mingled with the Edinburgh literati. Many had already heard of Pringle's recent arrival in the city and were looking forward to meeting him. Mr Foote became quite giddy introducing him to everyone and declaring him a 'delightful, most vivacious and joyous companion'. It was at this supper that he was invited to attend, as the guest of Hume, a meeting of the Poker Club, where they dined, conversed and played backgammon. Whilst there, he was asked if he might like to join a gathering of the Select Society the following evening. Not only did he attend, but he heartily contributed to the debate topic: 'Whether or not the Practice of Duelling be Advantageous'. He had never spoken quite so publicly before, and he had acquired a taste for it. He was asked not only to attend the following week but also to choose the topic for discussion, and had enthusiastically proposed 'The Condition and Treatment of Women'. He was looking forward immensely to contributing to the debate.

Whilst attending the Select Society, he was invited by a fellow member to join the Oyster Club the following day. And so it went on. Since his transformation he was rarely home, always well fed, well heard, well liked, and his opinions respected. As Pringle, he found he could barely walk down the street without a 'Good morning, Pringle! How are you this fine day?'

'Pringle, I hear you play backgammon as well as you debate!'

'Pringle, good man, come and join us at the Royal Exchange for some fine coffee and even finer discussion.'

'Pringle, join us for luncheon.'

Quite determined to enjoy the experiences put before him, Pringle had replied to every invitation with a hearty yes.

Katherine had also introduced him to one William Creech (whom Pringle had met many times in his previous life), a distinguished Edinburgh publisher who expressed an interest in perusing Pringle's poems, with a view to considering them for publication. It was all quite remarkable, but exhausting nonetheless, particularly for someone of his years.

Despite his fatigue, he realised he had never felt so vital and so confident in his opinions and his demeanour. He reflected that there had been moments in his life of intense loneliness when he had been unheard, and the voices in his head had become loud and voracious critics. He had been stifled by social convention, so much so that a thick cloud of scepticism had veiled his mind and made him profoundly unhappy. But in this convivial company, the veil did not have a chance to settle. For the first time Pringle felt that he was seen, known, admired even, and suddenly his thoughts were of interest to others. His contribution to the arts was now quite possibly worthy of publication: could he allow himself to believe this might happen? He must consider, however, that if one's ideas were praised too highly one might become a little conceited. He shook away this gloomy concern and focused instead on the overwhelming feeling that, yes, it was true: he had, quite simply, never felt so content in his life.

'Yes, Katherine, I am happy,' he said. 'A little weary, perhaps. But happier than I have ever been.'

'Well then,' she said, turning to face him, 'I think you need not dwell on the so-called morality of your actions. The core of who you are hasn't changed, it's just been allowed to flourish. The good Lord sees all. He sees the truth of who you truly are, and He will be pleased that you can now achieve the life you deserve. Your attire didn't change that. It is other people's perception of you that has shifted – shifted because you are a man. Consider the morality of *that*!'

Pringle nodded. 'You are so wise, dear Katherine,' he said, linking her arm under his own and looking out of the carriage with a smile.

Chapter 19

Robert Walker's introduction to his sermon, in the surroundings of the ancient kirk, gave Pringle a jolt. To his dismay, its subject was 'The eyes of the Lord are in every place', but given his discussion with Katherine in the carriage he tried hard to ignore the personal significance. Instead, he threw himself into singing with gusto as the congregation gave a rendition of 'God Moves in a Mysterious Way', and tried to shut the thought of an all-seeing God well and truly out of his mind. But still it lurked there, like a dark cloud, and put him slightly on edge. Nevertheless, he could not help but thoroughly enjoy the luncheon with the Walkers and their five young children at the nearby manse. It was a most convivial affair; the Reverend and his wife were attentive and kindly hosts, making Pringle and Katherine feel as though they were friends of old. Mrs Walker held their youngest, still an infant, in her arms while the other children, aged from two to ten, sat around the table in their finest clothes, delighting the guests with their easy affection and bright-eyed enthusiasm.

Pringle observed that the Walkers' eldest daughter Magdalen, who looked about seven or eight years old, took a particular shine to Katherine. After luncheon, when she had grown tired of the adult discussion, she had been allowed to get down from the table and began bringing her toys one by one from the nursery to show her new friend. Katherine was affectionate with the little girl and sat her on her knee, stroking her long hair.

'Do you have children or grandchildren?' Magdalen asked.

Katherine shook her head. 'No,' she said brightly, but with a tender stroke of Magdalen's face. 'That wasn't to be for me. But you can pretend, if you like,' she added.

Magdalen smiled and put her arms around Katherine in a most gentle hug. On her next trip back from the nursery, she held a shawl-wrapped doll carefully in her arms.

'And who is this?' Katherine asked, peering at the child's precious bundle. The face of the doll was wooden, with ruby lips and a crown of soft, curling black hair.

'Baby Martha,' whispered Magdalen. 'She's sleeping,'

she added, rocking the doll back and forth. She gently raised her finger to her lips in a 'shh' gesture and Katherine nodded and smiled.

Suddenly, Magdalen's older brother John announced loudly, 'That doll is a boy!' He was a robust-looking child of about ten years old, the oldest of the Walker children and, thought Pringle, a boy who took his role of second man of the house seriously. 'He's a man, actually,' he continued. 'He's called Lord Greyling. If you were to look under the swaddling, you'd see his breeches and velvet jacket.'

Undeterred by this outburst, Magdalen cocked her head to one side and pouted. 'Hush, John. You'll waken baby Martha with all your shouting.'

At this, John stood up, a mottled sprawl of purple rising up his neck to his cheeks. 'Lord Greyling isn't a baby girl. He's a fine gentleman!'

'It's my doll, John, and I can call it whatever I like,' said Magdalen resolutely.

'It's not your doll!' said John, with a stamp of his foot. 'He was a gift to all of us. Mother, Father! Look what's she done to Lord Greyling!'

'What does it matter, John?' said Walker calmly. 'Magdalen can dress the doll as a baby if she wishes to. She is doing no harm.'

'But it's not just that he's a baby,' wailed John. 'It's that she's made him a girl! It's wrong to make a boy a girl. God intended for that doll to be a boy, and what Magdalen is doing is wrong in God's eyes.'

Pringle, observing this unfolding drama, wondered if his own face had come to match the colour of John's. He shifted uncomfortably in his seat and glanced at Katherine, who rolled her eyes. In disapproval of him, of John, or of God himself, Pringle wasn't entirely sure.

Robert Walker turned to his son. 'Do you remember what my sermon was about, dear boy?'

'Yes, Father,' said John, his face earnest and attentive. 'That God sees all.'

'A young minister in the making!' said Katherine, with a broad smile towards Pringle. He smiled weakly back, feeling himself sinking into his seat and into himself. He fiddled with his spoon.

'Indeed,' said Walker.

'So God sees what Magdalen has done,' said John, 'and he will be cross with her.' He pulled a pious face in the direction of his little sister.

'Ah, but don't you think God sees past the clothes?' said his father. 'God sees who is underneath the simple garments we wear to keep us warm and to show our status to the world. Even underneath the physical traits that make a man or a woman. He sees through all of that!'

'He sees our bones and our blood?' said Magdalen.

'He sees right through to what we cannot see,' said Walker. 'He sees the soul. And it is the goodness and righteousness of the soul that is important. So, whether that doll is Lord Greyling or baby Martha, as long as the godliness and goodness shine through, nothing else matters. Not the clothes, not the physical traits, just the soul.'

Pringle realised he had forgotten to breathe during the entire conversation. He pulled himself up to a normal sitting position.

'I see, Father,' said John, contrite but still chewing his lip with annoyance at his little sister, who now rocked baby Martha with something like defiance.

'Martha is a very good baby,' said Magdalen. 'I don't think God would be cross with her.'

'No, indeed,' said Katherine, wrapping her arm around the little girl's shoulders. 'Baby Martha is indeed quite innocent in her slumber. Perhaps it is time to put her in her cradle.'

Mrs Walker smiled. 'A very good idea, Miss Hume,' she said, relieved.

Magdalen smiled sweetly. Holding Martha like a precious piece of china, she began to creep quietly out of the room. But just before she disappeared, she threw John such a look of triumph that Katherine had to stifle a chuckle.

'God sees all, Magdalen,' muttered John, at which

his father patted him on the shoulder, and everyone laughed, Pringle possibly the loudest.

'Let us have a change of scenery,' announced Mrs Walker with a smile. 'A walk, before dusk is upon us.'

Everyone stood up from the table and Katherine took Pringle's arm as they left the dining room. 'I think this visit has given you the good Lord's approval,' she murmured.

'If it is sufficient enough for baby Martha, it is sufficient enough for me,' said Pringle, taking his hat from the stand.

The watery daylight was swiftly diminishing, and they ambled carefully from the manse down the narrow lane towards the whitewashed cottages and tiny harbour of Cramond, where they stood for some moments looking out across the frosted beach towards the Forth and the boats sailing over towards Fife and beyond.

'What a peaceful spot,' said Katherine.

'And the air is so clean and fresh,' added Pringle, taking in a lungful.

The children, free of caution, shrieked with excitement when they found a piece of frozen water large enough to slide along.

'Father!' called Magdalen, her cheeks and nose pink with cold. 'We are skating, just like you!'

Pringle smiled at Walker. 'Where did you learn to skate?' he asked.

'My father took a post in Rotterdam soon after I was born, so as a lad I learned on the frozen canals,' the minister said cheerfully. 'Wonderful, wonderful skating there. It was possible on those long, sparkling ice roads to attain a terrific speed.'

'It is certainly a most invigorating pastime.'

'Indeed. It is always a delight to make the acquaintance of someone who shares this passion. And so, before I forget, I must give you this.' He pulled a white envelope from the inside of his jacket and handed it to Pringle, who, frowning, slid a gloved finger under the seal and broke it to reveal an invitation. The card was thick, and stamped with the Edinburgh Skating Club emblem, two skates intertwined with the words *Ocior Euro*. 'That means—'

'Swifter than the east wind,' Pringle interrupted with a smile.

Walker nodded. 'We consider you a most suitable candidate for the club, and would be delighted if you would join us. This is just the trivial little business of a demonstration, by you, of the requisite skills. At Duddingston next Saturday – the last Saturday before Christmas!'

Pringle swallowed. 'How perfect,' he stammered.

'Unless of course there is a thaw, but that looks unlikely for the moment,' said Walker briskly. 'I took the liberty of noting the moves on the back of the invitation, to give you the opportunity to practise, if you really need to,' he added, patting Pringle on the back.

'Thank you,' said Pringle.

'Not at all, my good man,' said Walker.

At this point, luckily for Pringle, although unfortunately for the child, Magdalen lost her footing and she fell heavily, landing in a crumpled heap on the hard ice. She threw back her head and howled. Whilst her parents comforted her, Pringle had time to regain his composure and begin to consider how much practice he could do before the demonstration at Duddingston. He flipped the invitation over and saw a carefully scrawled list. The first test was just as he had thought: a complete circle on either foot. But then he felt rising panic, as he saw that between him and the medal he aspired to was an almighty, literal hurdle. He had known he had to perform a jump. That in itself had sounded so benign. *A simple jump*. And yet the thought of it had made his ankles quiver. Pringle now knew he needed a miracle if he were ever to become a member of the Edinburgh Skating Club, for to succeed he had to achieve the impossible: he had to jump not over just one hat placed on the ice, but three. He felt the flames of his ambition beginning to gutter, smothered by his own fears.

'What's the matter now?' said Katherine, holding the baby whilst Mrs Walker tended to Magdalen. 'You look ill. For the umpteenth time today, may I say.

I thought we had established that God has given you His blessing.'

Pringle rolled his eyes. 'Oh, Katherine,' he said, glancing down at the list on the card in his hand, 'what the good Lord giveth me with one hand, He taketh away with the other.'

Chapter 20

21st century, Edinburgh

Claire Sharp couldn't sleep. That in itself wasn't entirely unusual these days, but the trip to Drumlanrig had unsettled her. Despite her decision to end her association with Peter, she had been mulling over all the information they had gathered during that visit: the missing 'real' Raeburn portrait of the Reverend Robert Walker, unlikely to be found; the close friendship that never was between Raeburn and Walker. These all suggested that the painting hanging in the National Gallery was highly unlikely to be a Raeburn. And then there was Jen's curveball suggestion that in fact it might not even have been Walker in the painting at all. That one in particular had sent her into a spin.

But most unsettling of all had been the text from Peter. Jen had tried to convince her that there was a simple explanation for his knowledge of her movements, and for the most part she accepted that. She reminded herself that she could be alarmingly forgetful these days, so much so that she increasingly doubted herself. She had racked her brain trying to remember exactly what had been said at that meeting with Peter in the National Gallery and whether she had mentioned in passing that a trip to Drumlanrig might be on the cards. What remained, though, was a churning sense in the pit of her stomach that she hadn't said a word about it and that he knew by some perfidious means.

Peter hadn't phoned as she had hoped the following day, which had prolonged the anxiety, but essentially it was over. It was a relief not just because of the paranoia and sense of doom, but because she knew she couldn't commit to this level of untruth. Her integrity as an art historian was at stake, and if the university were to somehow hear of her covert investigations she would surely lose her job. No, the deal was off. It was a blow, as the money would have been useful and possibly essential, in view of a chain of emails doing the rounds alleging that university cuts were looming, but accepting what was essentially a bribe to lie – or at any rate to assert something she did not know to be true – about a painting's provenance was wrong. And she knew it. But as she didn't have any way to contact Peter, she had no choice but to wait for him to call her.

Claire swung herself out of bed and wandered through to the kitchen. She mindlessly raked around in her cupboard and discovered an old jar of Ovaltine at the very back. She pulled off the lid and scraped a spoonful of the congealed contents into a mug, then poured on some cold milk, poked the lumps around and placed it in the microwave.

Her phone buzzed. She jumped, and glanced at the screen. It was Jen; she should have known, since she was really the only person likely to be up at this time of night. The text said *Call me*.

Claire touched the image of Jen smiling on the screen.

'Lordy, I didn't mean immediately,' said her friend. 'Sorry, did I wake you?'

'No,' said Claire, 'I was awake. Actually, I can't sleep.'

'Have you tried counting skating ministers?' said Jen. 'I find that works.'

Claire chuckled. 'Mmm, I should try it. I've been seeing that bloody image every time I close my eyes.' The microwave pinged and she opened the door to see a steaming mug which had boiled over. 'Ugh,' she said.

'Positive thoughts,' said Jen.

'No, no, it's not that,' said Claire. 'The milk has just boiled over. So anyway, why are you awake in these wee small hours?' She put Jen on loudspeaker and began mopping up the milk.

'I've been doing some research. Actually, I had a very pleasant trip to the National Library today. I was there all day, and managed to do some reading. And . . . wait till you hear this. Our minister friend in the painting may not just have been having a spontaneous skate one frosty morning. He was probably a member of the Edinburgh Skating Club. It was an actual thing. Lots of fairly distinguished gentlemen in Edinburgh were members of clubs at the time: the Oyster Club, the Poker Club and so on.'

'I think I knew that . . . vaguely,' said Claire.

'Well, fortunately, the Edinburgh Skating Club kept very neat and tidy records, and I found a splendid little book that lists all the members and their professions, way back to the birth of the club in the early seventeen hundreds.'

'Gosh,' said Claire, still trying to deal with the spilled milk. 'I had no idea.'

'It was a highly organised sport, with them all skating together like a display team,' Jen continued. 'I mean, ridiculous, really. Anyway, I scoured the pages and I haven't found Raeburn or any other artists who were members at the right time, so I'm pretty sure our minister wasn't painted by a professional.'

'Right,' said Claire. 'And I've found absolutely no

evidence in the style to connect it to any other Edinburgh-based portrait painters anyway.' She sighed. 'So I think maybe we should just move on. I just feel uncomfortable about the whole thing. There's something about it that makes me feel . . . oh, I don't know, a bit grubby somehow.'

'Yes. Well, too late for that, oh grubby one,' said Jen bluntly. 'You've got me hooked, I'm afraid. I can't put this one down. It's got me completely gripped.'

'To what end?'

'No end. We don't need to tell anyone,' said Jen. 'But I feel there's something there that needs to be found.'

Claire sighed. 'I know what you mean. But I think we've reached a dead end, in terms of the artist.'

'Well, I think we're going to have to widen the net in this investigation and perhaps not see dead ends as a negative.'

'Me? Negative?' said Claire, rolling her eyes.

'A cul de sac means a wrong turn. There's a wealth of other roads out there. Look, hear me out. The Reverend Robert Walker is the only minister listed. Amongst the professions of our funny gentlemen skaters were sol-icitors, judges and surgeons, all rather stiff and boring, but there was one member who was listed as a writer. That in itself stood out: an arty type in amongst all the professionals, as it were, So I thought I'd see what I could find out about him.'

'Oh, yes?' said Claire as she decanted the lumpy Ovaltine into another mug. She was beginning to wonder why she'd bothered. 'Go on,' she said, and took a sip. She grimaced. It was foul.

'Well, this guy sounds rather interesting, actually,' Jen continued as Claire tipped the contents of the mug down the sink. 'I cross-referenced him in the archives of other gentlemen's clubs of the time and it turns out he was listed as being a member of several – not just as a member but as a guest at some dinners. However, I couldn't find any evidence of his written work.'

'Okay,' said Claire, wondering where this was leading.

'So I went back to the skating club, and guess what? According to the records, each new member of the skating club had to be nominated, and who do you think nominated this chap? Our very own Reverend Robert Walker!'

'Okay, that is amazing. But I don't understand what you're driving at. Are you saying *he* could be our painter? I thought you said he was a writer.'

'Possibly,' said Jen. 'But he was quite the character, it seems. Charismatic and flamboyant. Something of a showman, perhaps. There are even a few references to him in the newspapers and journals of the time, not that I've studied them all yet.' She paused. 'Claire, do you get where I'm going with this? Perhaps *he's* the gentleman in the picture.'

There was a silence.

'Look,' Jen continued, 'I know it's a bit of a long shot, but he sounds like someone who wouldn't have objected to being captured in that way, and he also sounds like someone somebody out there would have wanted to paint.'

'But he wasn't a minister, Jen,' said Claire. She sat down at the kitchen table and rubbed her brow.

'Why does he have to be a minister?' said Jen, her voice sounding a little tense. 'Look at the picture again. It could just be a man in a frock coat with a neckerchief.'

Claire reached over and grabbed the book of Raeburn's portraits that was lying on the table under a pile of papers. It fell open at the page of the skater and she studied the picture. It was true. The coat and trousers looked black, but that could have been the lighting or indeed the age of the painting. They could have been a very dark midnight blue.

'What did you say his name was?' she said.

'Pringle,' said Jen, sounding as though she was rifling through a notebook. 'Yes, here it is. Mr Francis Pringle.'

Chapter 21

'Dr Sharp?'

Claire pressed her phone to her ear, took a sharp intake of breath and slowed down. She had recognised his voice instantly. She had a free afternoon and was heading towards the National Library, where she had arranged to help Jen in her research into this intriguing Edinburgh gentleman, Francis Pringle. The streets were busy with tourists and she was having difficulty navigating the narrow pavements.

'Good morning, Peter,' she said.

'I was wondering if we might have a chat. Is this a good time?'

'Erm, well,' she stammered, 'I'm actually on my way to meet a colleague. But I'm glad you called. You see, I've had a good hard think about your proposal, and I just don't think I can see it through.'

There was silence until several buses roared past her.

'I'm sorry, Dr Sharp, the line is a little noisy. I didn't quite catch what you said.'

'It's a no, I'm afraid.' She was shouting a little now. 'The proposal. I can't continue.'

'I see.'

'Whilst I agree that the painting is very unlikely to be a Raeburn, I now don't think it will be possible to back up that theory with any hard evidence. I've spoken to a colleague who thinks that the missing Raeburn painting, the accredited one of Robert Walker which might help prove the theory, is long gone. But the real reason is that I don't believe it's a Danloux painting either.'

Silence again.

'Peter? Can you still hear me?' Claire paused. Now well along Forrest Road, beside Greyfriars kirk, she took a step into the cemetery entrance.

'That's very disappointing, Dr Sharp,' she heard him say. Then he broke up a little, but she caught odd words: ' . . . of the deal . . . isn't enough . . . most displeased . . . rescinding our agreement.'

'Sorry, I can't hear you very well, Peter, but I should remind you, I didn't sign a contract,' she said mildly.

'It was a verbal agreement, Dr Sharp.' This she heard as though he were standing beside her.

'What? Oh, come on,' said Claire. 'That's a bit silly, is it not? I said I'd think about it.' She could see tourists merrily gathering around the statue of Greyfriars Bobby, posing for selfies and rubbing his nose. Someone was wrapping a scarf around his neck.

'I have a recording of our conversation, Dr Sharp.' Peter's voice had changed. It was flat and cold. 'You are obliged to complete your part of the deal.'

'I have completed it,' said Claire. 'I've thought it over, and I think you'll find I'm not obliged to do anything.'

'I don't like being let down, Dr Sharp,' said Peter.

'I beg your pardon?' said Claire. Had she really heard correctly?

'Dr Sharp, I urge you to reconsider, or things might not go well for you.'

'What? What on earth are you talking about? I'm hanging up now.' She took her phone away from her ear and ended the call, shaking her head in disbelief.

She was still shaking her head when she arrived at the library. Jen was waiting in the foyer. 'I think I've just received a threat,' Claire told her.

Jen listened intently as Claire filled her in on the conversation with Peter as they climbed the stairs. 'Blackmail too,' she said, wide-eyed. 'I feel a bit responsible. I didn't think it would lead to anything like this; it just seemed like a bit of fun. Don't you think you ought to tell the police?'

Claire shook her head. 'I'd feel a bit stupid. And

there's nothing really to report. Peter might not even be his real name. Do you know, it just sounded so far-fetched and ridiculous, I really couldn't take him seriously. It was as if he was saying lines he'd heard in a film, or a TV cop drama. Let's just forget it.'

Her phone began buzzing again.

'Oh, what now?' she groaned. 'More threats?' she said as she answered the call.

'Claire? It's Eleanor Strange.'

'Oh, Eleanor,' said Claire. 'Sorry, I thought you were someone else.'

'I hope you're sitting down,' said Eleanor, taking no notice. 'You're not going to believe this.' Her voice sounded unusually breathless.

'No, I probably won't. What is it?'

'That painting,' said Eleanor. 'The one we were discussing the other day, the missing one of the Reverend Robert Walker by Henry Raeburn? I think we might've found it.'

'What?' said Claire. She stopped dead on the stairs.

'Remember I said these things aren't found, they simply emerge? Well, it would seem the time was right.'

When Eleanor ended the call, Claire stared wordlessly at Jen for a moment. Then she reached out and put her hand on her arm.

'What is it?' said Jen.

MICHELLE SLOAN

'I don't believe it,' Claire said. 'The missing painting could be right here in Edinburgh!'

Chapter 22

'It's completely and utterly extraordinary,' said Claire.

She was standing with Eleanor and Jen in the iconic 'Black and White corridor' of the General Assembly Hall situated on the Mound, the hill that snakes up from Princes Street to join the Royal Mile. Here, the annual meeting took place of the General Assembly of the Church of Scotland. And there on the wall of this grand corridor, in amongst several other dusty portraits, was a man in ecclesiastical robes, possibly in his forties, his hands clasped together. He had a large aquiline nose, a high colour and lively eyes that gazed out at his viewers, quite oblivious of the storm that was now brewing. The only definite physical similarity between himself and the skater was the grey hair, except this appeared to be a wig.

'How do we know, though?' Jen asked, peering upwards. 'The plaque says it's the Reverend Gilbert Hamilton. How on earth do we disprove that?'

'Right. A couple of things,' said Eleanor. She pulled out a notebook and leafed through some pages, referring to her notes. 'The Church of Scotland archives are all held elsewhere, so I've had to do rather a lot of delving and I've only got so far. However, this painting *is* listed in the archives as a Raeburn, right enough, so that's a start, but there is no title or name given. It was gifted by an anonymous donor in, wait for it, 1896. So that fits nicely with the auction in Edinburgh.'

'Gifted? Why?' said Jen.

'An act of piety?' Claire suggested. 'To ease a troubled soul?'

'The wealthy can buy their piety if need be,' said Jen with a nod.

'And there was no record of who the sitter was in the archives?' Claire asked.

'No, most annoyingly,' said Eleanor. 'So let me explain my theory. It would seem that at some point after the General Assembly received it, it was labelled with an incorrect name.'

'Why Gilbert Hamilton, I wonder?' said Jen.

'Well, it would all fit rather neatly if one were to take an educated guess based on the context. Gilbert was also a minster at Cramond kirk, like Walker, but – and here's the clincher – he was a Moderator of the Church of Scotland, an individual held in very high esteem, so it was an easy assumption to make.'

'Right, so forgive me for being stupid, but why is it *not* him?'

'Well,' said Eleanor with a smile, 'this is where I put my Miss Marple hat on. Gilbert Hamilton actually died at the age of eighty in 1787, the very year Raeburn began painting portraits in Edinburgh. It was the year he opened his studio here.'

'This man doesn't look eighty. He looks much younger than that,' said Jen.

'In his forties or early fifties,' said Claire.

'Exactly. It really *can't* be Gilbert, who would have been an old man when Raeburn started painting professionally. So it must be Walker, as the sale room listing suggests.'

'That's incredible,' said Jen.

Claire bit her lip. 'It's not a watertight case,' she said, 'but it's still very exciting.'

Eleanor nodded. 'Yes. We could do with something written, though, just to back it all up.'

'I wish we could take the painting down for a closer look. It's tucked up so high it's hard to get a decent view of it. It certainly looks as if it needs cleaning.'

'Well, good luck with that.' Eleanor sighed. 'It was hard enough getting access to this corridor.'

'Bit of luck finding it,' said Jen. 'Like finding that needle in the haystack.'

'Were you just toying with us at Drumlanrig, Eleanor?' Claire asked. 'Did you know all along it was here?'

Eleanor allowed a slight smile to curl her lips. 'Nope. Actually, it was something you said, Jen. Something we art historians omit in our sleuthing.'

Jen raised her eyebrows.

'You wondered *why* it was purchased. That it was perhaps for more than value, collectability or mere pride of possession. That it was purchased for sentimental reasons, or out of a strong emotional connection or sense of respect. Somebody might have purchased it *because* it was a minister.'

'Okay, but how did you work out it would end up here? In this most unlikely of locations,' said Jen, looking around.

'I asked myself two things,' Eleanor began. 'First, and very simply, where might there be a lot of paintings of ministers?' She waved her hands around her. There were indeed ministers wherever they looked.

'And then,' she continued, 'I began to think about paintings hanging in such obvious locations that they become invisible. So much a part of the furniture and the bricks that they are seen but never *observed*. A corridor seemed a good place for that. Which led me here.'

'In plain sight,' Jen murmured.

'Superb work, Eleanor,' said Claire. She reached into her bag for her phone. 'I think I'll make some quick calls. First to the Church of Scotland to say that the portrait needs cleaning, but at some point I'll have to give the National Gallery a bell as well. They ought to know about this.'

'Be warned,' said Eleanor. 'They may not *want* to know about it.'

Claire smiled. 'Oh, they'll be extremely miffed to hear their precious skating minister isn't a Raeburn after all.'

'What will they do with the enormous cardboard cut-out, I wonder?' said Jen. 'I think it would look rather nice in my living room.'

Claire left Eleanor and Jen chuckling in the corridor and glanced at her phone. There were many texts, all from Peter. They began as mild messages, but as Claire scrolled through them she realised they were increasingly hysterical. And threatening.

And then the phone began to ring. It was her boss.

'Brian,' she said, pressing the phone to her ear.

'Claire, good to have caught you. Can you possibly pop in to see me this afternoon, around half two? Look, I'm not going to beat around the bush. I'm afraid I've had a rather unsettling email.' His voice was strained.

'Oh?'

'Yes. It's from a gallery in London, accusing you of accepting a bribe to misidentify a painting,' said Brian.

'What?' said Claire. 'Brian, what are you talking about?'

'They have a recording of you, Claire, and phone records. It's pretty serious stuff. I can't sugar-coat it.'

'I'll see you at half two, Brian', she said, and hung up.

Chapter 23

I t's not true,' she said. 'The recording you just played me has been doctored in some way to make it *sound* as though I'm accepting a bribe. And how exactly did it come to be in this gallery's possession?'

Brian raised an eyebrow. 'I took a brief call from one of their employees, a Peter Henry, who said this recording was given to them by one of their clients. They feel it is their moral duty to let the university know, which is why they forwarded all the details.'

'No! That man, or boy, Peter approached *me*,' said Claire, her voice a little louder than she had planned. Then she shut her eyes at the horror of her own admission. 'He's behind it all.'

Brian sighed. 'Okay, time to fill me in, Claire. What the hell happened?'

'Right, okay, I did briefly speak to this man Peter

about the possibility of identifying a painting as a Danloux, not a Raeburn,' said Claire. 'He phoned and asked to meet me. I realised it was dodgy, of course, but the money was a huge temptation, with everything that's going on here and cuts and so forth. But I didn't do what they asked, and now he's punishing me by making it sound as though I did something unethical.'

Brian frowned and folded his arms. 'Which painting was it?' Claire sighed, and Brian closed his eyes in anguish. 'Oh, please, not the Skating Minister, for crying out loud?'

'Look, this is just his clumsy way of getting back at me,' said Claire. 'He clearly wants you to sack me.'

Brian sighed. 'I probably ought to,' he said.

'How long have you known me, Brian? I'm not a criminal.'

'It appears to be quite a distinguished gallery in Mayfair, Claire. And these are quite influential people. If this were to get into the press . . .'

'But they're lying,' Claire insisted. 'Or he is.'

She looked at the emailed document on Brian's screen. It was signed by P. Henry on behalf of the gallery owner, whose name was not mentioned. It was all too perfect. She grabbed her phone and googled Peter Henry and the gallery's name. No matches. Then she googled the gallery. It didn't exist.

'Phone them,' said Claire. 'Go on. Phone them.'

'There's no number on the email,' he said. She watched as he typed into Google.

'Right, so that's strange,' he said. 'There appears to be no Peter Henry art dealer and no Londaux of Mayfair. What were you thinking even meeting with this guy? God knows who he is.'

'I know, I know,' said Claire. 'It was stupid. So, so stupid.' She ran her fingers through her hair. 'The money was ridiculous too. Way, way too good to be true.'

'Don't tell me any more,' said Brian, his hands raised in horror.

Claire stared at the gallery heading on Brian's screen. *Londaux*. 'Oh, wait,' she murmured. She could feel heat rising from her neck up to her scalp. She grabbed a pencil from Brian's desk and scribbled the letters on a scrap of paper.

'Oh, Jesus. Peter Henry Londaux?'

Brian frowned. 'I don't follow.'

'Don't you see? It's a sort of anagram. For Henri-Pierre Danloux!' She began to laugh.

'Claire, this really isn't funny. I think we should call the police.'

'God, no!' said Claire. 'I'm mortified enough as it is.'

Brian stared at her. 'But he's obviously some sort of scammer.'

Claire nodded. 'Oh yes. And a blackmailer. Oh, and I think he's managed to track me on my phone too.'

'Could he be violent?' Brian was looking anxious.

'A violent Danloux enthusiast? For goodness' sake, now I've heard it all. No, Brian, I don't think he's dangerous. He looks like a kid. I'm pretty sure he's just a fantasist and a bloody wee chancer.'

'Well, you never know.'

Claire began to chuckle again. 'Wait till I tell Jen,' she said. 'She'll love this.'

Brian rolled his eyes. 'Thank God I didn't sack you. And that the press didn't hear about it.'

'But there is something of interest out of all this,' Claire said, calming down. 'It's led us to believe that a Raeburn painting hanging in the General Assembly has been mislabelled and is in fact the missing portrait of the Reverend Robert Walker.'

Brian stared at Claire as he processed this latest bit of information. 'Oh, no, Claire, please let's not rake up the whole Skating Minister thing again.' He sounded exasperated. 'It's far too contentious an issue.'

'But, just wait until you hear this.' She filled him in on the details, and finished: 'Look, there are other professionals who will back me up. Eleanor Strange, the curator of Drumlanrig, has been working with me on it. And Jen Brodie, of course.'

'But it's a big claim, Claire,' said Brian. 'This isn't something we can keep out of the press.'

Claire shook her head. 'No, but it would be quite a

coup for the department if we could prove that the portrait in the Black and White corridor is an actual Raeburn painting of the Reverend Robert Walker,' she said. She sensed he was coming round to the idea.

'You're sure?' he said.

'Pretty much. But it needs closer examination and a clean,' said Claire. 'It would be good to get it down off the wall for closer inspection before we say anything to the folks at the gallery.'

'Okay, but you'd better be right about this,' said Brian. 'I'll make some calls. Looks like your Danloux fan got his wish after all.'

'Well, possibly. We'll see,' she said. 'The National Gallery might just settle for its being a Danloux, but I have my doubts.' She stood up and put on her coat.

Brian smiled and shook his head. 'Never a dull minute, Claire, never a dull minute.'

'Just keeping you on your toes, Brian. Thanks for being so understanding.' She was just about to leave the office when he called her back.

'So, if that painting in the National Gallery isn't the Reverend Robert Walker, who is it? And if it's not a Danloux, then who painted it?'

'Ah,' said Claire. 'We're working on that.'

Chapter 24

18th century, Edinburgh

As the skaters of Edinburgh hoped, the freezing weather retained its icy grip on the city, and now, in mid-December, the daylight hours were scant and precious, which suited Pringle in his quest for undercover practice. He had taken to regular early morning visits to the frozen lochs of St Margaret's and Duddingston, but now that time was running out before his 'skills trial' and the dreaded jump, his practice sessions had become something of an obsession, and he returned later in the day for further work, until the pinkish gleam of a frosty sunset gave way to the pale rising moon.

It was late afternoon, and Pringle, who was battling

with a persistent head cold and fighting the urge to stay cosy by a roaring fire, was just about to head off for Duddingston when there was a knock at the door. He opened it to see Katherine and a small boy with bright red hair, a button nose covered in freckles, and a pair of ice skates slung around his neck.

'Why, Katherine!' he said. 'I was just about to leave for an afternoon skate.'

'Indeed, and we are coming too,' said Katherine brightly.

Pringle frowned. 'Katherine, dearest, you have a small boy with you.'

'Ah,' said a conspiratorial Katherine. 'This isn't just any small boy. This is Squirrel.'

'Squirrel?' said Pringle.

'John Macnutt,' said the boy, reaching out his tiny hand. 'A pleasure to meet you, Mr Pringle. Everyone calls me Squirrel.'

Pringle put out a hand, whilst wiping his nose on his handkerchief with the other.

'Squirrel is a most excellent skater,' added Katherine. 'He has agreed to help you with your practice. This boy is your secret weapon.'

Pringle, his eyes watering profusely, stared down at the lad. He was smiling, revealing missing front teeth, and he had very large eyes, so that with his tufty hair he looked more like an owlet than a squirrel. He could only have been about seven years old, maybe not even that.

'I see,' said Pringle. 'And where did you find Squirrel, Katherine?'

'Mr Foote and I took a little jaunt to Lochend the other day, to procure you a tutor. Lo and behold, there we found a whole gang of tiny skaters,' she said breezily. 'Squirrel and I fell into conversation, and I simply asked if he might like to earn a little money.'

Squirrel nodded enthusiastically.

'I see,' said Pringle. 'You seem rather young, laddie. Are you any good?'

'Just you wait,' said Katherine.

Pringle frowned. 'Well then, we must get going.'

'Bring a pillow or two, sir,' said Squirrel. 'And we need some string.'

'What on earth for?'

'So you don't get hurt, sir,' said Squirrel, his eyes unblinking.

Was this a threat? thought Pringle. 'I see,' he said.

He supposed he could see the sense in this. He had taken to wearing as many layers of clothing as he could conceivably get away with, not only for warmth but in order to cushion his falls, but still he was covered in bruises. He did as he was instructed and grabbed two pillows from his bed and a large ball of string from the pantry.

They set off in the carriage, not quite a merry party of three, but a party of three nonetheless, heading out to Duddingston. Pringle felt apprehensive with this new little companion sitting opposite him, staring, and tried to stare back, only to receive an audacious smile and a wink. The boy was downright impertinent! Pringle shifted uncomfortably in his seat. He was quite sure this child was going to make mincemeat of him on the ice.

Katherine, meanwhile, gazing out of the carriage window, looked extremely pleased with life. She had, resting on the seat beside her, a satchel full of pencils and chalks, a roll of paper, a wooden board and even a small stool. She often accompanied Pringle on these outings, not only out of loyalty and a wish to give wise words of encouragement, but also because she had taken to sketching and drawing outside. She had explained that she loved a reason to be outdoors, to observe the changing colours. The light, she had said, was quite exquisite, the ice creating an otherworldly glow. Mainly, she sketched with pencils and chalks outdoors, adapting or reworking her sketches using oil paints on returning home. Then she could dab and swirl to recreate the palette of pale wintry shades of the icy loch that were imprinted on her memory.

'Will you draw young Squirrel here?' Pringle asked.

'Perhaps,' said Katherine. 'But as it happens, I am

working on a fine portrait of you, Francis,' she said. 'Skating gracefully across the ice. Actually, that reminds me . . .' She reached into her satchel and pulled out a pair of tiny silver scissors. 'Would you be kind enough to give me a lock of your hair?'

'I suppose so,' said Pringle, a little confused. 'For what purpose?'

'Your hair is quite an unusual colour and I need to mix my paints to match it exactly,' she said. Pringle noticed that a slight flush came to her cheeks as she said it.

He reached over and took the scissors from her hand, then reached round to the back of his neck and pulled a small section from under the clubbed hair at the nape. 'Will this suffice?' he said.

Katherine nodded a little shyly. He snipped, then passed the coiled hair and the scissors back to her, and Squirrel rolled his eyes.

'When will I get to see this painting?' said Pringle, ignoring Squirrel.

'Ah, well, I have decided that you can have the painting as a reward – a memento – when you join the Edinburgh Skating Club,' Katherine told him. 'You've been working so hard.'

'Katherine, that is so kind of you. I do hope it is a true depiction of my skating experience so far, complete with gritted teeth, arms whirling like a windmill, legs like a newborn foal's, mostly on my backside and not forgetting a bulbous red nose with a drip on the end.'

Squirrel laughed a little too hard at this, but Katherine patted Pringle on the knee.

'Not at all, my dearest,' she said. 'It shall be a most dignified and elegant pose, like an arabesque.'

'Something to aspire to then, I suppose,' he muttered.

Katherine frowned a little. 'I've not quite mastered your hat. For some reason that's being particularly troublesome, but other than that it is shaping up to be a portrait of a most impressive skater.'

Pringle smiled and rolled his eyes. 'Who the devil are you painting, then? Surely not me!'

'You may not believe me, Francis, but sometimes you look rather accomplished as you glide across the ice. And I think I've captured your poise rather well.'

Pringle let out a chortle. 'Accomplished? Poise? That I would like to see.'

'Well, you shall not see it until it's finished and you have that medal round your neck,' she said firmly. 'And then we shall have a little celebratory soirée.'

Pringle smiled at this. Like most women, Katherine had been tutored in art as a young girl and had developed a flair truly worthy of admiration. But once completed her paintings became like most women's creative contributions: quiet, private and unseen. Pringle, however, thought her a most proficient artist, and often told her so. He had seen some of her lochside sketches, in which she had captured other sights as well as himself. They often shared the ice with shinty players, scuttling around chasing their ball, or curlers sliding their flat stones towards the mark. Hot chestnut stalls popped up on the shore on busy afternoons, and the odd military band added musical accompaniment to the merriment. At times, it was truly joyful.

But joy wasn't enough to overcome the immediate challenge facing Pringle this evening: to leap over not one, but three hats stacked in a tower. It wasn't so much the leap that filled Pringle with abject terror – it was the prospect of landing.

Chapter 25

Squirrel didn't waste any time on their arrival at Duddingston.

'Tie the pillows around your waist, sir,' he said, and went off to put on his skates. Katherine helped Pringle arrange the pillows carefully around his hips so that he had one protecting his front and the other secured firmly to his behind.

'Oh, Katherine, I am too old for this,' he protested. 'I fear I am taking it all too far! I am full of this blasted cold and I'm afraid I will break an ankle and it will all be a fiasco.'

'Come, come, now, Francis.' Katherine wagged a finger. 'It's just a sniffle. Don't use this as an excuse. You don't want to turn up at Duddingston on Saturday and make a fool of yourself, now, do you? Squirrel will sort you out, mark my words.'

Pringle turned and watched as Squirrel glided off. It was a sight to behold. This tiny wee boy with his fiery red hair shot around the loch like a demon, leaping and sliding, soaring and spinning, as though the activity were as natural to him as walking or running.

'That lad is remarkable!' said Pringle. 'Quite remarkable.' He stepped out on to the ice, and immediately lost his balance and fell. But as he slapped against the ice, he realised there was no pain. In fact, he was completely pain free, thanks to the cushions.

'What are ye doing, Mr Pringle?' said Squirrel, swooping down on him and hauling him back up to his feet. 'No lying around. Let's get to work!'

Despite his young age, Squirrel was a precocious individual. As Pringle began to demonstrate his simple skills – a figure of eight, followed by a circle on each leg – Squirrel buzzed around him, adjusting his balance, barking commands, reminding him to 'Keep yer chin up, sir!'

'Stop leaning back, sir!'

'Stop leaning forward, sir!'

'Yer doing it again, sir, no staring at yer feet!'

But then they had to achieve the impossible. Pringle had to learn how to jump. Squirrel demonstrated, landing so smoothly that his pupil almost growled in frustration.

'Bend yer knees, sir!' shouted the lad, demonstrating

a crouch so low his behind was skimming the ice. 'Right doon!' But it was no good. Pringle stumbled, he staggered, he slithered, and every time he lifted his feet off the ice by even an inch, he ended up flat on his back looking up to the stars above.

'Yer no going fast enough,' said the boy, shaking his head in disapproval. Showing off now, he skated past his reluctant pupil at speed, bent low, and then, using his arms like windmills to help propel him upwards, he leapt into the air. He landed low, his behind stuck out, his chin up. 'See? Try to keep your eyes up, Mr Pringle. Dinnae look doon!'

Pringle nodded stiffly. 'I'm trying my best.' The frustration was building. He could feel himself getting more and more annoyed with the boy.

'Dinnae be feart,' called the lad. 'I've watched ye. Yer a scaredy cat – a feartie!'

Pringle frowned. 'What did you just call me?' He had been called many things in his life, but never a feartie. It was outrageous!

'Squirrel's quite right,' shouted Katherine from the bank. She was peering over the board which held her sketch, a jute cloth apron tied over her warm coat. 'Yer a feartie, so ye are!' She mimicked Squirrel's voice.

'You've got to go *fast*,' said the lad. 'Yer no a namby-pamby lady, yer a man!'

Pringle gritted his teeth. Why were they ganging up

on him? He was becoming annoyed.

'Bend yer knees right doon when ye take off, Feartie Face, and even lower when you land.'

'Stop calling me Feartie Face,' said Pringle. 'I don't like it!'

Squirrel laughed. 'I'll stop calling ye Feartie Face when you stop being one.'

Pringle was furious now. He wanted to give the boy a cuff for his impertinence. 'Call me that again, laddie, and I'll wipe that smirk off your face.'

But then Squirrel went too far. He skated close to Pringle, leapt up, wheeched his hat from his head and shot off.

'Catch me if you can, Feartie,' he cried, and with the hat clasped in his hands he turned and skated away as fast as his tiny legs would go. Infuriated by the challenge, Pringle sped off after him. Adrenaline and anger pulsing through his veins made him skate faster than he had ever done before. It was truly exhilarating and terrifying at the same time.

'Ye'll no get me,' called the boy a few moments later, 'but ye might get over the hat.'

Then he flung the hat behind him right in Pringle's way. Horrified, Pringle realised he had no choice but to jump to avoid it: there was no time for anything else. Instinct made him hoist up his arms and leap, and before he realised what he was doing he landed squarely with his knees bent low, his chin up. He couldn't believe it. He was still on his feet.

From the bank, Katherine cheered.

'Ye did it, but only just!' shouted the boy. 'Again, again! Ye'll never manage three hats unless ye go faster and higher!'

Pringle swished round and repeated the move another ten times at least. Each time he began with a chase around the loch after Squirrel yelling insults at him.

'This boy is a scurrilous fellow! Where on earth did you find him, Katherine?' Pringle cried, whizzing along the ice.

'His other nickname is Wee Nick!' shouted Katherine. 'For he certainly looks like the devil on ice!'

But devil or not, he certainly helped Pringle master the blasted jumps. He soon added a second hat, which Katherine, unbeknown to Pringle, had brought with her. And an hour later, pillows removed from his waist, and another hat borrowed from a benevolent gentleman, Pringle could finally jump all three. This had Katherine on her feet, clapping and cheering, and teacher and pupil skated over to join her.

'Well, lad, you've certainly done a marvellous job!' she said, giving him a hug. Her nose was red, as were her cheeks, and in the hue of the sunset she looked, Pringle considered, quite the most healthy and glowing he had seen her in a long time.

'What about me?' he said. 'It's not an easy job, may I tell you.'

'There you go,' said Katherine, giving Squirrel some coins from her purse. Then she gave his face a tender brush with her hand.

'Thank you, miss,' said a beaming Squirrel. 'Pleasure to do business with you. Good luck, Feartie Face. I'll come and shout at ye for yer skating test, if the payment is right!' And with that, he turned and sped off once more over the frozen loch, skating ferociously towards the hot chestnut stall at the other side of the loch.

'I've got to hand it to you, dearest,' said Pringle, taking Katherine's hand and wrapping it into his own. 'You certainly know what's best for me.'

'I think we make rather a fine team, don't you?' she said, turning to pat his cheek affectionately.

Chapter 26

21st century, Edinburgh

'I think there's something obsessive about that painting.'

Jen was sitting at Claire's kitchen table. It was a dreich, wet Sunday afternoon and she had come round to sit with Claire during the dreaded open viewing of the flat. She was nursing a cup of tea in her hands, and in front of her was the book of Raeburn paintings. It was open at the portrait of the Skating Minister.

'What on earth do you mean, obsessive?' said Claire, who was attempting to declutter the kitchen work surfaces by stuffing everything out of sight into a cupboard. 'You're sounding, dare I say it, like an art historian.'

'I don't mean to sound pretentious. It's just my opinion,' said Jen, looking up over her glasses. 'I know I'm not artsy fartsy, but this feels as if it was painted by someone who had an eye for every single detail. Not in the sense of being a meticulous painter, but an eye for the detail of the skater. Of the man himself.'

'Are you saying it was painted by someone who was obsessed with the subject?' asked Claire, her head in the cupboard.

'I don't think I'm being literal in that sense,' said Jen. 'Actually, maybe I am. But if we're breaking down the absolute beauty of this painting, it's because everything about it is really sheer perfection.'

'Apart from the hat,' said Claire. 'Don't forget that bit.'

'Well, yes, that's obviously been repainted,' said Jen. 'I wonder why?'

The buzzer interrupted their conversation, and Claire trotted out of the kitchen to lift the handset.

'Yes, do come up,' she said, pressing the button and then opening the front door. 'But even the hat follows your logic, actually, Jen,' she said, coming back into the kitchen. 'In that why did he feel it needed repainting at all?'

'Yes, indeed.' Jen took a sip of tea. 'You always say he,' she remarked.

'What?'

'You always refer to the artist as "he",' said Jen, still peering down at the painting. 'Is it outwith the realms of possibility that it was a woman who painted this gentleman?' Then she looked up at Claire with something of a mysterious glint in her eye.

Claire frowned. 'Um . . .'

'Hello?' said a voice in the corridor.

Claire stuck her head round the door into the hall. 'Hi there,' she said. 'Do just have a good look round. I'll be in the kitchen if you have any questions, and there's a pile of schedules in the sitting room. Help yourself.'

Jen looked up from the book. 'Who is it?' she mouthed quietly.

'I think it's maybe a mother and son,' whispered Claire.

'Are you not going to give them a tour?'

Claire rolled her eyes and shook her head. 'I did all that at the beginning,' she said. 'And now, frankly, I just can't be bothered. I think they can work it out. It's hardly palatial; I mean, it's all pretty self-explanatory.'

Jen smiled. 'I take your point,' she said.

'You just feel ridiculous, you know,' Claire continued. 'And here's a cupboard, and here's another cupboard. I just let them do whatever.' She waved her hands.

Jen looked back at the painting. 'You know something else that strikes me?' she said. 'The feet.'

'What about them?' said Claire.

'They're very small,' said Jen. 'And those red ribbons

or ties on the skates are rather flamboyant for someone dressed so correctly.'

'Yes, I see what you mean. I hadn't really thought of that,' said Claire, leaning over the book. 'Maybe that's the way they came when you bought them, though. I mean, maybe everyone's skates looked like that. Remind me what we know about this man you think it might be.'

'Francis Pringle. It's well documented that he was very much part of the Enlightenment "in" crowd. He was a member of the Edinburgh Skating Club. Briefly.'

'What do you mean *briefly*?'

'Well, it seems he was listed as a member in the December of 1790. Actually, there's a really wonderful mention in a broadsheet from the time about him doing the skills test thingy at Duddingston. But he doesn't appear in the yearly lists before or after. It's the same with some of the other clubs. There's a tiny mention of him chairing a debate on the treatment of women at the Select Society.'

'Interesting,' said Claire.

'I believe he was an acquaintance of David Hume, Mr Enlightenment himself. By absolute chance I found a brief mention of a Mr Pringle in a letter written by Hume, saying he was staying in his apartment as a guest. I'm assuming it's the same Pringle.'

'So he wasn't actually from Edinburgh?'

Jen shrugged. 'Perhaps not.'

'So let us hypothetically move forward with this theory,' said Claire. 'Which of his Enlightenment chums was also nifty with a paintbrush? I guess we've ruled out any fellow members of the skating club.'

'Well, that's what we need to find out,' said Jen. 'But that's what I meant about his appearance being brief. What we see with references to Mr Pringle is that he appears in the archives several times within a very short space of a few months. And then nothing.'

'He dies?'

'Possibly,' Jen mused. 'That would be the obvious answer. But I can't find anything to support that.'

'What about the old parish death registers, or graveyards?'

'Nothing yet,' said Jen. 'I'll keep looking. Maybe he just went back to whence he'd come.'

The flat viewers shuffled into the kitchen, and Jen continued to study the painting while Claire began to show them round.

'There's an abundance of storage,' she said breezily. 'Cupboards here, and here too,' she opened doors above and below, 'and even a pantry . . . a press,' she added, opening a large door to reveal shelves. Then she glanced over at Jen, who was smiling and nodding her head in pretended interest.

'Thanks,' said the woman. 'I think we've seen everything. We'll let ourselves out if that's okay.'

'Of course,' said Claire, and made a face at Jen as they turned to leave. Within seconds there was another buzz from the entry system.

'As one cupboard door shuts, another one opens,' said Jen as Claire went out of the kitchen.

She didn't even speak into the intercom this time, but simply pressed the buzzer to release the street door. 'Well, they were just thrilled with the place, weren't they?' said Claire, returning to the kitchen.

'They didn't seem too enthusiastic, I must say,' Jen agreed.

'Hello?' a voice called from the hall.

'This could be the one,' whispered Jen, punching the air.

Claire walked back into the hall, and stopped.

Standing in the corridor of her flat was Peter.

Chapter 27

'What the hell are you doing here?' Claire snapped.

Peter looked a little bit different this time. The main thing was his hair. It wasn't smoothed down with a lard-laden comb as it had been previously but was now quite the opposite: a bit fluffy and unbrushed. Slightly damp from the rain, it seemed to point in all directions. He was dressed in jeans and the anorak he had worn at the National Gallery, but it was zipped up to his throat, and with a rucksack on his back he looked as if he was off to school. Give him a pair of shorts and a catapult and he'd give Dennis the Menace a run for his money.

'Look, I just wanted to speak to you,' he said, putting out a hand. His glasses had begun to steam up.

Jen appeared at the kitchen door behind Claire. 'Who's this?' she said.

'This, Jen, is Peter Henry, our Danloux enthusiast. And he's just leaving.'

'Jesus,' Jen gasped. 'Shall I call the police?'

'No, wait. I wanted to apologise,' Peter stammered. 'It really just started out as a dare that got out of hand.' He took off his glasses and tried to wipe them on his jacket pocket, but there wasn't enough dry fabric to do the job properly so he abandoned the attempt and slid them back on his nose.

'You could've had me sacked, you little shit,' said Claire, her anger rising. 'I almost called the police when I saw that email you sent to my boss, and I might still.'

Peter, who seemed a little alarmed by the wrath of the two women, began to shuffle backwards. 'I know, I know,' he said. 'That wasn't me, it was my mate. He took it all way too far.'

Claire glared at him. 'You know, you look familiar, but I can't place you,' she said.

Peter bit his lip. 'I really am called Peter. I was one of your students a few years ago. Not a very good one. I did Art History for a year, but kind of dropped out after second year.'

Claire folded her arms. 'Really?'

The door buzzed again. She reached over and lifted

the handset, pressing the button to release the main door downstairs.

'Witnesses,' she said pointedly. 'Just in case you're here to finish us off.'

Peter smiled weakly, his face flushing. 'I did a semester of Scottish History too, Professor Brodie. I liked your seminars.'

'Right. But clearly not mine,' said Claire. 'And moving on, so what now? You go about aggressively championing neoclassical painters?'

'No, I work in a bookshop. And I'm a delivery driver for Asda too,' he added with a note of pride in his voice.

'Oh well, that makes everything just fine, doesn't it?' said Jen.

A couple appeared at the front door, and walked in hesitantly.

'Hello! Do come in! You can wander freely.' Claire gave them a broad smile. 'Schedules are in the living room, ask any questions.' Her face dropped as soon as they were out of sight. 'You were saying?' she said between gritted teeth. 'Your little dastardly plan? For what purpose?'

'No. I – well, *we* – kinda thought it up as a bit of a dare and then it got well out of hand. Me and my mate Olly. He failed Art History too.'

'Oh, for God's sake,' said Jen in disgust.

'So what was it?' said Claire, trying to keep her voice down. 'Revenge because I failed you?'

Peter sighed. The couple viewing the flat came out into the hallway and everyone instantly stopped talking.

'Don't mind us,' said Claire. 'This young man is very keen on the flat.'

Peter let out a nervous laugh.

The woman smiled faintly and then squeezed apologetically past Jen and into the kitchen.

'You once said,' began Peter in a strained whisper, 'or rather announced, during a tutorial you held in the Beehive—'

'Oh, God.' Claire buried her face in her hands.

'. . . that if someone offered you enough money – because as an academic you were always skint – you could make a strong enough case for the reattribution of just about any painting. Within reason obviously. I mean, I don't think you meant *any* painting. That would be totally wild.'

Jen burst out laughing. Claire glared at her.

'So, a few months ago, after a couple of bevvies, Olly and I came up with this scheme,' Peter continued. 'We thought we'd give it a go and see how far we could take it. It was just a bit of fun, but then Olly got all heavy about it. I was never happy about pretending we could pay you, but Olly kept saying it was your fault for boasting about it in the first place. He was pretty pissed off with you for giving up on the whole thing. But actually, we're really sorry. Well, I am. Honestly.'

The couple reappeared in the hall again. 'We've seen enough,' said the man, raising his hands in something like surrender. 'Thanks, though.'

'Oh,' said Claire. 'Do you need me to answer any questions, or—'

'No, thanks!' The woman waved quickly, without looking back, and then they were gone.

'Damn,' muttered Claire. 'That's your fault.' She jabbed an accusing finger towards Peter. 'They couldn't get out of here fast enough.'

'It's four o'clock, anyway,' said Peter with a weak smile. 'You can relax now.'

'Well, thank you very much. How did you know where I live, anyway?' spat Claire irritably. She pushed past him to shut the front door.

'Er, well, I was kind of tracking you,' he said sheepishly. 'I set up an app thing that can do that. Remotely. It's probably a wee bit illegal. And then I realised this was your flat and it was for sale and then I checked the viewing times and I thought I'd just come and see you face to face and explain. I live just round the corner, as it happens,' he added brightly.

Claire stared at him. 'Wait a minute. So that's how you knew I was at Drumlanrig Castle,' she said. 'I *knew*

I hadn't told you I was going there. I thought I was losing it!'

Jen shook her head. 'What were you thinking?' she said. 'Stalking, blackmail – I mean, that's enough for an arrest. And did you ever ask yourselves what would have happened if Dr Sharp had fallen for your bribe? You could *all* have ended up in prison.'

'I know, I know,' said Peter. 'It all got out of hand. Look, you may not believe it, but I'm really sorry, and I've brought you a peace offering.'

He rummaged around in his rucksack and pulled out a bottle of wine.

Jen raised her eyebrows.

Claire kept her arms folded.

Jen reached out and took the wine.

'Well, I suppose it's not been an entirely wasted exercise,' said Claire.

'No, indeed,' said Jen, examining the label with approval. 'I'll fetch the corkscrew,' she added, disappearing into the kitchen.

'I didn't mean *that*,' said Claire, following her. Peter shuffled into the kitchen behind them. 'I meant that this little dare of yours and Olly's has unearthed something rather interesting, Peter.'

'Really?' said Peter.

Jen took out three wine glasses and poured them all a healthy measure.

'Well, as it happens, it turns out the Skating Minister isn't a Raeburn,' said Claire.

'And,' said Jen, handing Peter a glass, 'the minister isn't a minister.'

Peter took a large gulp of wine.

Chapter 28

18th century, Edinburgh

Pringle sat in front of a roaring fire in his flat, a blanket wrapped around his shoulders, his throbbing feet soaking in a chamber pot filled with steaming hot water. His head ached and he now had a streaming cold. The events of the last few weeks, it seemed, had finally caught up with him, and he now felt so achy and tired that he was close to weeping. A sharp rap at the front door sent an unaccustomed feeling of dread washing over him.

'Come in,' he croaked miserably.

The door opened and there was Katherine, resplendent in a long green wrap with a fur trim. Her hair was beautifully coiffed, with an ostrich feather sweeping up and over from the back of her head.

'Dearest Katherine,' sniffed Pringle, opening his eyes a little wider. 'You look quite wonderful!'

But Katherine's face quickly dropped into a thunderous expression. 'What are you doing?' she said, her long pearl earrings dancing in the firelight. 'You are not dressed! We should be on our way to the ball. The carriage is waiting for us on the High Street.'

'I don't think I can make it. This cold is awful, my feet are aching, and I feel utterly wretched.'

Katherine sighed. 'But it's the very first ball at the Assembly Rooms on George Street. It is the most important occasion of the year. Everyone will be there in their finest!'

'And with you looking so elegant too, my dearest, I shall look like a sack of tatties beside you.'

Katherine swept past him and into the bedroom, where she began moving clothes around.

'I think your velvet jacket and green knee breeches would be appropriate,' she called through to him. 'A change from your dark jacket, which is far too ministerial for my liking. I trust you have shoes suitable for dancing. You won't be allowed into the ball wearing boots.'

'What are you doing?' he groaned. 'I said I wasn't coming.'

'And I say you are,' replied Katherine firmly, coming back into the sitting room.

'What?'

'Francis Pringle, I have supported you every step of the way on this little experiment. I have given you encouragement when you have faltered. I have introduced you to a prominent publisher – I have even procured you a skating teacher. It is time you repaid me.'

'By going to a ball?'

'We are to mingle with Edinburgh's elite. We shall dance and be merry together!' said Katherine grandly.

Francis groaned. 'No! I just can't do it. My feet are sore, so is my head, and my throat is on fire. I am wrung out. You can go with your brother, I am sure.'

Katherine folded her arms. 'I am fifty-five years of age, Francis,' she said calmly. 'For all those years I have attended balls and social gatherings with my brother. I've endured looks of pity: the spinster who cannot find a husband. I have progressed through unbearable social gatherings, year after year, as a plain and unwanted creature. I have put aside my own humiliation for the sake of propriety. And now I am written off as an old maid. Never in my life have I had the pleasure of a man on my arm: a man who is attentive and charming; a man who not only wants to be with me, but with whom others clamour to be in company. To go tonight with you, the toast of Edinburgh, would ensure that for once in my life I am regarded as something of value – of value to someone other than my own kin. I would like that

189

experience, and, goodness me, you of all people should understand that! You owe me this, Francis.'

Pringle stared at Katherine in awe. There was a long pause. He sniffed.

'Well, I see,' he said. 'I've never heard you speak with such determination, Katherine Hume. And of course you are completely right.' He shrugged off the blanket. 'I fear I have been very selfish. I would do anything for you, my dearest. It would be an honour to escort you to the ball.' He took his feet out of the pot and gave them a shake. Then he stood up and made a stiff attempt at a sweeping bow.

Katherine smiled. 'Thank you.'

'But I think you would not like me to be on your arm dressed in an old nightshirt, so I must excuse myself,' said Pringle, hobbling towards the bedroom. 'Oh, but I do feel quite wretched.'

Katherine closed her eyes and bit her lip. 'You have a cold,' she said. 'In all the years I have known you, you have dismissed colds as a mere trifle, a sniffle to be shaken off. You have laughed at men who have taken to their beds at the first sneeze. But now you seem to be somewhat dramatising it yourself!'

Pringle nodded, then closed the door.

'A glass of punch will no doubt shake off those aches,' Katherine called.

'I think you are right,' said Pringle through the door.

'I feel a little better just for putting on these fine clothes.'

Katherine rolled her eyes. 'Do you not remember the dance you once held in your flat?' she said. 'How we pushed the furniture to the walls, and the fiddler was almost out of the window, but what merriment, what happiness!'

'Yes, yes!' cried Pringle. 'Two and twenty persons were dancing in my little abode! A happier occasion I cannot remember.'

After a few minutes he opened the door, now dressed in all his finery. He walked forward and put his arm out to Katherine.

'Will I do, dear Katherine?' he asked.

'Yes,' she said with a smile. 'Apart from your swollen red nose and watery eyes you will do very well indeed, Mr Pringle.'

'Shall we?' he said, opening the front door. And off they went, down the stair and into the night.

Chapter 29

Pringle was just removing his cape and gloves and handing them to a waiting footman when he noticed that Katherine was deep in conversation with Captain Jamesson, the rather pompous Master of Ceremonies of the Assembly Rooms. She came scuttling back, quite glowing.

'Oh, my dear, we have been asked to lead the minuet,' she said, her hand to her heart. 'The very first dance of the evening!'

'Are you sure?' Pringle stammered, whilst nodding and smiling to someone he vaguely recognised from one of the many clubs and societies he had been attending.

'Yes. Captain Jamesson just told me that you and I have been chosen to be the first couple to dance!'

'But why?' said Pringle, frowning. 'I hope you didn't accept.'

'Oh, for goodness' sake! Of course I accepted,' she snapped. She opened her fan and began wafting her face excitedly, then closed it with a swift jerk. 'Think of what this means, Francis!' Not only have you been accepted into the bosom of Edinburgh's literati; you are considered to be the most distinguished gentleman here.'

'Well, not just me, Katherine,' said Pringle. 'You also, dearest. But who on earth put us forward? We can't possibly do it. It's extraordinary.' He shook his head in disbelief, pondering the mystery of who might have nominated them.

Katherine took no notice. 'Never in my life did I imagine I would be given such an honour,' she said, beaming with delight and completely ignoring Pringle, who attempted to protest.

'I do understand it's something of an honour, but really . . .' he began, but Katherine wasn't listening. She had seen someone across the room and was waving to her.

'Everyone gets a little nervous about these things,' she said briskly as she hurried away to spread the news.

'A little nervous?' Pringle repeated to himself incredulously. He was beginning to feel faint. It was dawning on him what it would actually mean. The eyes of five hundred people would be upon them! And if he were to stumble, or forget what he was supposed to be doing, their little 'experiment' would be instantly over. The shame! The shame! He was consumed with terror, and beads of sweat began to form on his forehead. He felt feverish again. He tried to think through the steps of the minuet, but his mouth was dry, and his mind began to race wildly.

'If I'd known, we could have squeezed in a little rehearsal,' he said aloud, but no one was listening. He slapped a hand to his clammy forehead and closed his eyes.

When he opened them again, he could not see Katherine anywhere. She was doubtless chatting, smiling and preening to all and sundry. Whilst Pringle fretted she mingled, with ease and delight, not in the least concerned. Pringle conceded to himself that he needed help. Again. He scanned the room until he spotted Foote – the very person! Foote was chatting animatedly to a group of ostentatiously dressed young men. He fixed a smile on his face and negotiated his way through the crowds until he was at the actor's side. Foote was wearing a grand powdered wig, and rather a lot of white face paint and rouge.

'Excuse me, gentlemen, may I borrow Mr Foote?' Pringle asked politely.

'Pringle, my dear man!' boomed Foote, giving him a low bow. 'Isn't this just delightful? The chandelier, the ballgowns! The twinkle of the candlelight on every face, pearly bosom, gleaming button, glittering brocade and bejewelled lady here. The room is positively shimmering, as if it were made of cloth of gold. And I hear you and dear Miss Hume are set to lead the dancing in the minuet!' Then he gave Pringle a knowing wink.

Pringle felt his face begin to twitch. 'You!' he said. '*You* put us forward?'

'Wasn't that clever of me?' said Foote with a broad smile, snatching a glass of steaming negus from a passing tray. 'Actually, it was Miss Hume's idea.' He then took a sip of the spicy port, smacking his lips. 'I just spoke to the right people. You and your beautiful partner will be the belles of the ball. The talk of the town! If that wasn't an accolade to your new identity, I don't know what is!'

'Mr Foote, I haven't danced a minuet in years,' said Pringle urgently. 'And as you can imagine' – he looked around to make sure no one was earwigging – 'I might need a little tuition in the male part.'

Foote laughed raucously. 'I must admit, I hadn't thought of that,' he said. 'I don't think we can rehearse together now, Mr Pringle. That might rather cause a stir. Besides, you worry too much, man.' He slapped Pringle on the back, slightly winding him. 'Fear not! It will be spectacular!' He gave a little jig and then swept off, shouting a greeting to someone across the crowded room.

Pringle grimaced.

He just needed to practise, he thought, trying to calm his racing mind. He set off to look for a room where he wouldn't be disturbed. Mercifully, the card room was empty.

Pringle placed himself in the middle of the room and took a deep breath. He lifted his feet and began to count out loud, marking out the steps. He put out a hand to an imaginary lady as he swept around in the curves of an S.

'Remember to offer your right hand, not your left,' said a voice, making him jump. It was Mrs Agnes McElhose, in all her finery, who stepped forward out of a dark corner.

'Why, Nancy! I mean Mrs McElhose!' said Pringle in surprise. 'Forgive me, I was just reminding myself of the steps! I didn't know anyone was in here.'

'It is I who should apologise,' she said with a smile. 'I was awaiting a . . .' she paused and bit her lip, 'a friend, but you dance so well, I felt compelled to comment!'

For one terrible moment, Pringle felt her eyes lingering on him for rather too long, and he wondered if she recognised him. But then she lifted the fan she was holding up to her face and peeked at him coyly over the lace trim.

Just then the door burst open and Foote marched in. 'He's here!' he shouted, and Katherine rushed in and came face to face with Mrs McElhose.

It was a most peculiar moment. Katherine's bright face instantly soured, and without acknowledging Nancy she stepped forward and took Pringle's hand as though he were a naughty schoolboy.

'We are about to begin,' she said, glowering at Mrs McElhose, and with a dramatic sweep she led Pringle out of the room. 'What were you doing in there?' she asked under her breath as they returned to the ballroom.

'Practising,' said Pringle. 'I had no idea Nancy was in there until she revealed herself.'

'Oh, I'll wager that woman knew you were there!' Katherine snapped.

'Katherine!' blurted Pringle, almost laughing at this extraordinary outburst. He stopped and gently turned her to face him. Her cheeks aflame, she could barely meet his eyes. 'What on earth are you saying? Why are you so angry? Nancy is one of our dearest friends. She was waiting for someone – Mr Burns, I shouldn't wonder. They're always having some sort of conspiratorial tête-a-tête.'

Katherine sniffed and looked away, leaving Pringle perplexed. Fortunately, this most confusing and vexing exchange was interrupted by Captain Jamesson, who asked them to take the floor: the minuet was about to commence.

Katherine regained her composure. 'Forgive me, Francis,' she said quietly. She shook her head a little. 'My nerves got the better of me.'

'Of course,' he said, but he glanced at her curiously.

'Well, 'tis time, most honoured couple,' said Foote, appearing at Katherine's elbow. He handed Pringle a glass of wine. 'Down this, it's medicinal. And then, dear ones, do take your places.' Pringle stared at the wine and then, in one swift movement, lifted it to his lips and knocked it back. The effect was instant; he felt fortified and ready for action.

Foote took back the glass. 'I almost forgot,' he said, and reached into his pocket to pull out an orange, which he handed to Pringle.

'Stow this in your pocket and remember to present Miss Hume with it at the end of the dance. She will be most impressed by your thoughtfulness.'

Pringle slid the orange into the pocket of his coat, touched by this small act of kindness. 'Well, thank you, Mr Foote. I wouldn't have remembered.'

Mr Foote smiled, and then, with a nod, he swept out his hand towards the dance floor and bowed a little. The crowd parted expectantly.

Pringle smiled at Katherine. 'Now then, dearest, let us give this our very best shot.' And he put out his arm and led Katherine to the centre of the ballroom.

Chapter 30

21st century, Edinburgh

Gullan's Books, an antiquarian bookshop sat towards the tail end of the Royal Mile, nestled surreptitiously between the entrance to Gullan's Close and an ice cream shop. Its window was so low it was almost touching the slope of the pavement and was covered with a somewhat intimidating metal grille. This monstrosity was presumably supposed to be removed during the day, but the padlock swinging on the side was rusted tight.

'There,' said Jen, pointing. 'That's what we're after. The caricatures.'

Between the bars, the display before them on the deep windowsill was almost invisible except for a backdrop of faded maps and a front row of cellophane-covered prints of slightly comical profiles. Claire had to crouch down to get a decent view of the pictures. There was a trail of dead flies scattered between them.

'Mmm. I think perhaps they need to work on their presentation a bit,' she remarked. 'This portcullis across the window suggests they want to keep us out rather than welcome us in.'

A face appeared through the window and waved to Claire. It was Peter.

'There's the baby-faced assassin,' she said.

Jen and Claire headed into the shop.

'Welcome!' said Peter awkwardly. He wasn't wearing his anorak this time, but a tight green sweater that emphasised his puny form.

'When you said you worked in a bookshop, I imagined something rather neat and clinical,' said Jen. 'But this,' she gave a wave of her hands, 'this is an emporium!'

The inside of the shop matched exactly what was suggested by the exterior. Piles, stacks and indeed mountains of books surrounded them. It had the feeling, smell and chaos of an attic used for storage for many centuries.

'It's a bit of a mess, I know, but we're in the process of sorting the stock and getting new shelves fitted,' said Peter apologetically.

Claire looked around, doubtful that any kind of order could ever be established.

'My boss isn't here today, so I can take a break,' Peter went on.

'If you don't mind my saying, you're hardly swamped with customers,' remarked Jen, looking around.

Peter ignored this and led them through the maze of shelves to the back where, hidden behind piles of boxes and yet more books, was something of an office. 'Please, er, take a seat,' he said, lifting books from a stool and a chair. 'Sorry about the . . . well, the books everywhere.'

'So, what have you got for us, Peter?' said Claire, planting herself down on the stool. Jen took the seat beside her.

'Well, you were talking about this chap Francis Pringle on Sunday, and how you thought he might have been a bit of an Edinburgh celebrity in his day,' he said, turning his back to them to rifle through the mass of papers on the desk. 'Ah, here it is.' He turned round to perch on the edge of the desk, holding a book. 'The prints I mentioned on the phone to you, Professor Brodie, are by an artist of the late eighteenth century.'

'The ones in the window,' said Claire.

'Yes, there are a few faded ones there; we're the only real stockist in Edinburgh,' said Peter. 'But there are many, many more. They're by a kind of caricaturist of the day – a man called John Kay. He was an etcher, and managed to capture some of the key characters of Enlightenment Edinburgh, doing, you know, everyday things. Not always in the most flattering of ways, I might add. He did some of the local townspeople, too. You know, the well-kent faces of the High Street.'

He passed Claire and Jen the book: page after page of profiles of men and women in eighteenth-century clothing. The images were black and white.

'He had a shop very near here, actually,' Peter went on, 'where he would sell his etchings and also watch the good folk go by. A bit of a paparazzo of his time, you might say.'

'You mean, they didn't like it?' said Claire. 'The people of Edinburgh?'

'No,' said Peter. 'Not really. Well, I suppose some took it in good spirit, but in fact some well-known figures were very unhappy when they saw his depictions and would rush to buy them so they could be destroyed before they were widely distributed.'

'So, what's this to do with our Mr Pringle?' said Jen.

'Well, I found one of him. In fact, I found two,' he said triumphantly. He reached out to retrieve the book and flicked through the pages until he came to one with a Post-it note sticking out.

'There,' he said with a touch of pride in his voice.

He passed the book back to Claire and Jen. Three figures were captured in profile, two men and a woman. Their postures were identical, as though they walked as one. The note beside it read *Mr David Hume, Miss Katherine*

Hume and Mr Francis Pringle. Three Noble Friends Walking the Dog. David Hume was portrayed as rather portly, with three buttons clearly popping off his waistcoat. Ahead of him was Katherine Hume, large-girthed and double chinned, at her feet a little Pomeranian with its tongue lolling out. And at the head of the line was the tall figure of Mr Francis Pringle, dressed from head to toe in black. All three, and the dog, were smiling as though sharing a private joke.

Jen looked up from the book and gave Peter a nod of approval. 'This is marvellous, Peter. Well done.'

'So, who was Katherine Hume exactly? A relation of the more famous David?' Claire asked.

'Yes, his sister,' said Jen. 'She lived with him, I believe, until his death. But I don't know anything else. I shall need to do a little delving.'

'But they're all rather good friends, it would seem,' said Claire. 'Even the title says so.'

'Yes. And there's another one. Pardon me,' said Peter, taking the book back once again and turning the page. This time it was just two figures, Pringle and Katherine Hume.

Claire looked at the picture. Once again the two figures stood side on, Pringle in front, striding forth, his posture upright and robust, whilst a small, dumpy Katherine walked behind him, seemingly trying to keep up. She appeared to be waving something at him.

'Well, I never,' said Jen. 'Just look what Katherine Hume is holding.'

In one hand, her thumb neatly tucked through the hole, she held a palette; in the other she held aloft a selection of paintbrushes.

Chapter 31

Claire and Jen left Gullan's Books and wound their way back up the Royal Mile, through the throng of tourists who were spilling out on to the road.

'The boy done good in the end,' said Jen as they passed St Giles' Cathedral. 'Don't you think?'

'Well, I suppose it makes up for it somehow,' said Claire. 'But this recent revelation begs the question, what about the women of the Enlightenment?'

'What do you mean?'

Claire stopped and looked around. 'On this stretch of the Royal Mile alone we've walked past statues of Robert Fergusson, Adam Smith, and now . . .' Claire pointed to the impressive statue that stood outside the High Court, 'here we have a semi-clad Greek god version of David Hume. But what about the women? Were their minds and thoughts and ideas really any "less than", "inferior to" the men's? Of course not. But it seems that at the time they were left on the fringes and then, over the years, essentially airbrushed out of one of the most significant cultural movements in history.'

Jen sighed. 'Absolutely. When you really begin to open your eyes to it all, it's so disappointing. I mean, there were women-only clubs and societies at the time, I believe, but as you say, it's as if their input had no real value. As if they were only operating on the periphery of the Enlightenment.'

Claire folded her arms. 'And now, it's as though they've been forgotten,' she said. 'So, Katherine Hume. The mere sister of this man.' She waved across to the statue once more. 'Did *she* paint her friend Francis Pringle skating on Duddingston Loch? I mean, why not? *Could* she have been such an accomplished painter? It certainly seems as though even a woman of such skill could slip under the radar and be forever in the shadow of her famous brother, both during their lifetime and beyond.'

'Why not, indeed?' agreed Jen. 'It must have been well known she painted, given there's a caricature of her holding paintbrushes. Women were tutored in art and music and racked up many "accomplishments". I guess on the whole they just weren't allowed to truly flourish.'

They stood together at the crossroads of the Lawnmarket and Bank Street pondering this. Pedestrians milled around them, and a piper stood nearby, belting out 'Highland Cathedral'.

'And I mean, look, even an Edinburgh thief gets an iconic pub in his honour,' said Claire, pointing to Deacon Brodie's tavern, named after the legendary Edinburgh cabinetmaker: distinguished craftsman by day and menacing burglar by night, hanged on one of his own gibbets.

'Well, quite,' said Jen, with a knowing nod. 'But on that bombshell, I think I shall leave you here, if you don't mind. I've got a few things I want to do before my afternoon seminars.'

Claire frowned. 'More research?'

'Perhaps,' said Jen. And with an enigmatic smile, she crossed the street to the rhythm of the beeping green man, gave Claire a backward wave and headed towards George IV Bridge.

Claire walked on down the Mound and back up towards the General Assembly, where she was due to meet Brian for a closer inspection of the Raeburn painting. It had been taken down, on Claire's suggestion and Brian's recommendation to the Church of Scotland, for cleaning and restoration. When Claire arrived, Brian seemed unusually excited. He was hopping up and down, leaning in close and then back again, his arms folded, examining the gloomy portrait that was propped against the wall. He also seemed to be in conversation with an officious-looking woman who Claire assumed, given she was clutching a bunch of keys, was someone from the Church in charge of the premises. Two men stood nearby, leaning against the wall and engrossed in their phones, presumably enjoying a break after having taken the picture down.

'Ah, Claire, you're here,' said Brian. 'Isn't this just marvellous? What a privilege to see it up close. In fact, to be quite honest, I've never really looked at it at all, but it really is quite something.'

Claire squatted down to have a closer look. What was she expecting to see? Yes, there was the familiar intensity of the Raeburn stroke. But of course there was no signature, and nothing to identify the sitter.

'Mmm. The varnish is extremely stained,' she said. 'Have you informed the National Gallery of our wee find?'

'Well, not yet,' said Brian, rubbing a hand over his chin. 'I think we should hang fire. The facilities department of the Church of Scotland really need to make the decision on that, and they were sticky enough about us getting it restored in the first place.' He said this last bit between his teeth so that the woman with the keys wouldn't hear.

'Surely the Church won't mind,' said Claire. 'I think

they'd be delighted if this is indeed the Reverend Robert Walker. He was an impressive individual.'

'Well, yes,' Brian conceded. 'But, you know, I don't think the National Gallery will be too over the moon to hear their precious poster boy's provenance questioned *yet* again. I think it's fair to say they would be extremely cautious at this stage.'

'You've spoken to someone, haven't you?' said Claire.

Brian sighed. 'Let's just say I made a speculative enquiry. I get the feeling they don't want to be involved at all until the identity of the sitter in this painting can be proved unequivocally. And I don't think it's likely that will ever happen, to be honest, without clear documentary evidence.'

Claire nodded. 'I thought they might say that.'

'I don't need to remind you that the last time someone questioned the Skating Minister a huge furore erupted,' Brian continued. 'Not just in the gallery itself. The public were raging that what is seen as an icon of Scotland was being impugned. I think the gallery's hoping it will all blow over again and nothing has to change. It's part of their brand, after all.'

'Oh, well,' said Claire sarcastically, 'that's fine then. Let's just keep lying to the Scottish people. Don't you think they'd rather know the truth?'

Brian ignored her and turned to talk to the woman with the keys.

'And even if we did prove it,' Claire continued quietly, still on her haunches staring at the bored-looking and black-draped minister gazing back at her, 'Danloux is conveniently in the wings to become the official painter of the Skating Minister. Except it's not a Danloux and it's not a minister. And, actually, it was possibly painted by a woman. I wonder how that will hit them?'

'Sorry, what was that?' said Brian, turning back. 'Were you talking to me?'

'Nope, just myself,' snapped Claire.

Brian didn't notice her tetchy tone. 'Do you know,' he pressed on, his voice light and breezy, 'I think we should suggest a Raeburn exhibition in the university. We've got several and the General Assembly would surely lend us this one. Rather than having them scattered around various buildings just hanging in gloomy rooms, I'm going to explore shifting them all to a more airy space so that they can be properly seen and the students don't have to go hunting for them. Maybe we could even connect with other faculties to have a "Figures of the Enlightenment" exhibition. You know, see if anatomy, law and anyone else want to get involved.'

Claire nodded in a noncommittal way. 'All the men together, eh?'

The official-looking woman had now been joined by the two men Claire had seen checking their phones, ready to lift the painting at each end and take it away to be packaged up and sent off to the restorer.

'Claire, you don't seem too thrilled,' said Brian. 'I mean, you were the one who brought this to our attention.'

'Well, it's good it's going to be restored,' she said, standing up. 'I just feel it's the key to solving the Skating Minister mystery. But there's a missing link in the chain – the documentary evidence we need to prove this is Robert Walker.' She smiled at Brian weakly. 'I don't know,' she said. 'I probably need to give it a rest now.'

'I'm saying nothing,' said Brian, his hands raised. 'I don't see how any of that really matters. I didn't the first time round, to be honest.'

The men reached a door at the far end of the corridor, and there was a bit of directional shouting as the woman with the keys had to unlock it. As the men turned to fit the painting through, the stuffy image of the minister disappeared and the back of the painting was revealed. Claire frowned. Something was chalked on to the surface. She felt her heart beat faster.

'Wait!' she shouted. She rushed forward and looked at the writing. *Lot 91* was clearly written in white chalk. 'Oh my goodness, just give me two minutes,' she said to the men. The woman with the keys tutted.

Claire reached into her bag, grabbed her phone and scrolled for Eleanor Strange's number. Fortunately, Eleanor answered instantly. 'Claire?'

'The painting from the Black and White corridor,' Claire told her. 'It has a lot number chalked on the back. Do you know, or know where we can locate, the lot number from the auction house, Dowell's, I think you said it was, in 1896?'

'Oh, yes, I've got that written down,' Eleanor said. 'Hang on.' Claire could hear her rummaging and then flicking through the pages of a notebook. 'Yes, here. November 14, 1896, Dowell's auction house in George Street, Edinburgh. "Portrait of the late Dr Robert Walker" by Sir Henry Raeburn, Lot 91.'

'Yes!' said Claire, gripping her hand into a fist. 'The missing link!'

Chapter 32

18th century, Edinburgh

'Auld Reikie,' sighed Pringle.

He was making his way home from the ball in the Assembly Rooms. Most people had travelled home in the comfort of a carriage, but Pringle had insisted that he would walk. He had just turned from the North Bridge back up the Royal Mile, and he now realised he was more at home with the squalor and the smog that was draped thickly over the crag and tail than he was with the grandeur of the New Town. As he walked, almost feeling his way in the darkness of the street, which was lit only by a handful of street lanterns, he mused over the words of his favourite poet, the brilliant, bohemian genius that was Robert Fergusson:

Auld Reikie! Thou'rt the canty hole, A bield for mony a caldrife soul . . .

And Auld Reikie had been his own cheerful place, his 'canty hole' at so many points in his life, a comfort in dark times. So too had it been his bield – his shelter, his protector, its great familiar and soothing arms wrapped around his soul. And now when he felt quite giddy with his momentary sense of success and fulfilment, he wanted to share his joy with his beloved city – to dance in the streets and closes themselves. He wanted to hold Old Smokey by the hand and dance a reel. Or perhaps a minuet! He skipped a few steps. Admittedly, he had over-imbibed, not as much as on St Andrew's Day but enough to feel just a little intoxicated. The alcohol had certainly helped his cold, the symptoms of which had quite dis-appeared, and had numbed his aching feet. He laughed to himself, savouring the moments of the evening he had enjoyed most. He and Katherine had shone, sparkled, even! Every pair of eyes in the ballroom had been on them as they had danced; they had been admired and lauded for their performance. So what if he had turned left instead of right at one point? It had not mattered one jot! In fact, he had corrected it with a neat little pas de bourrée which had received a fluttering of fans and an appreciative round of applause from a cluster of nearby ladies. At this, he had been so bold as to flash them a smile and a wink; he was quite the entertainer.

MICHELLE SLOAN

Katherine's little moment of anxiety in the card room had been forgotten, and she had been simply delightful thereafter. Foote's idea to present her with an orange after their minuet had been a stroke of genius. She had been quite enchanted by the small gift and had accepted it as if she had been presented with a fine jewel. She had, rather expansively, declared to those around her that the fruit was particularly succulent and refreshing, and seemed surprisingly keen to be observed as she devoured a segment.

After the minuet they had joined in several country dances, after which Katherine had swept around the room chatting graciously to many of the eminent guests. Later, Pringle had noticed her in deep conversation with the much-talked-about painter Henry Raeburn, who she later said had recently opened a studio in the New Town. He had agreed to help her fix the detail of the hat in the portrait she had been working on: Pringle himself skating on Duddingston loch. By all accounts he was quite charming, and most keen to help.

But for Pringle, what had been quite astounding was that so many fine individuals had actually *begged* to be introduced to him. He was in demand! As Foote had whispered to him, 'You are a rising star, Mr Pringle. You and Katherine are the glitterati of the literati!'

David Hume too had said, 'It would seem you are quite the man of the moment, Mr Pringle. You and

217

Katherine have made something of an impression upon the fine folk of Edinburgh. And every time I fall into conversation with a gentleman here, he doesn't wish to talk to me; he wishes to know you! I appear to be your gatekeeper.' He had then added, with his hand cupped to cover his mouth, 'I've shooed away some lesser mortals, dear Pringle!' at which they had both laughed uproariously.

But the highlight of the evening had been when William Creech had made his way over to Pringle to inform him that he would like to publish a book of his poetry, and would Pringle visit him at his bookshop in the Luckenbooths next week to discuss the matter further. Truly, he could not believe it. He was to be published. He really was to become a bona fide member of the Edinburgh literati. He would be remembered! Ramsay, Fergusson, Burns . . . and Pringle!

In short, the evening had been a rip-roaring success. Katherine and her brother had left first, as Hume was complaining of not feeling terribly well after consuming a gargantuan amount of food. He had remained at the Assembly Rooms until the wee small hours, dancing with many fine ladies and talking until his throat, already sore from his cold, gave up completely and his voice was almost inaudible. But his spirits were soaring, and his heart was bursting with pure happiness.

There was only one thing that nagged at him like a

small but persistent beastie picking at his brain. The skating trial was in but two days' time. It was, in his mind, the final hurdle. If he could just get that medal around his neck, then he would have succeeded! And as a stark and sobering reminder at the end of the evening, his new acquaintances assured him that they would all be there, cheering him on, on the banks of Duddingston Loch. Their intention was of course to be supportive, but Pringle felt sick at the mere thought of it.

'It will be fine,' he muttered aloud. 'All shall be well. And after a night like this, in my most beloved city, what can possibly go wrong?'

Just as he said this, he became aware that somewhere up above, muffled by the smog, a voice was shouting. His slow reaction was punished by a bucketful of slop, which landed on his head with a sickeningly wet thump and then proceeded to trickle down his hat on to his face and neck. By the smell of it, it was more than just cooking waste.

He let out a groan and took off the hat, attempting to shake off the worst of it. 'Oh, dear Lord,' he uttered, walking on, kicking nastiness from his breeches as he went. 'I do hope this is not some sort of omen.'

Chapter 33

21st century, Edinburgh

When Claire left the General Assembly she was feeling elated. The National Gallery had been informed of the latest turn of events and were already sending someone up to have a look at the painting and check out all the lines of evidence that Claire had outlined.

She had immediately phoned Jen to fill her in on the news, and in return, rather mysteriously, Jen had asked her to meet her near George Square, where the main buildings of the university were situated. She had said she wanted to show her something.

The sky had darkened, and as she walked the rain began to fall, so that soon she was negotiating her way along the narrow pavements through crowds of people brandishing umbrellas. She headed over George IV Bridge, past Chamber Street and down towards the student haunts of Potterrow and Bristo Square. Jen was waiting for her, sheltering under one of the university buildings, the hood of her anorak tight around her face. She gave Claire an 'onwards' wave and they set off at a quick pace towards George Square.

'Where are you taking me?' Claire asked.

'Ah, well, you were talking earlier about women of the Enlightenment – or rather the lack of them?' said Jen.

'Yes.'

'Well, that's what I want to show you.'

They carried on down the street, the cobbles shiny in the lashing rain, before taking a left along Windmill Street. At the corner where it joined Chapel Street, directly above the street sign itself, was a plaque. It was small, grey and rather drab.

'*Voila!*' said Jen, with a dramatic wave of her hand.

Claire read the inscription aloud. 'Mrs Cockburn who wrote *The Flowers o' the Forest* lies buried near here.' She glanced at Jen. 'That's it?'

'Alison Cockburn was one of the few documented female writers of the Enlightenment,' said Jen. 'She was also a good friend of David Hume, so presumably of Katherine too. She was, by all accounts, an absolute gem of a woman – her writing was respected by both Burns and Sir Walter Scott, whom she hosted for many a soirée in her flat. She sounds like our cup of tea. Or should I say our goblet of claret.'

'And this is all she gets?' said Claire bitterly. 'This pathetic, wee concrete plaque?'

Jen grimaced and shrugged. 'Sorry. It's a bit of a downer after your breakthrough today, but I thought you'd want to see it.'

Claire frowned. 'For a woman of the eighteenth century, all the wit and wisdom in the world gets you *this*. You wouldn't even notice it, it blends in with the concrete so well.'

She glanced at their surroundings. They were standing opposite the Pear Tree pub. Cars and vans trundled past through large puddles that were appearing by the roadside, drenching them as they went. 'Bloody weather just about sums it up.'

'Oh, this rain doth fall like a pathetic fallacy,' said Jen in a mock deep voice, giving Claire a friendly nudge.

Claire tutted, but there was a hint of humour about her eyes. 'Any further information about our Katherine Hume?' she asked, raindrops dripping down the end of her nose.

'Nope,' said Jen. 'Pretty much nothing so far. It's amazing how little there is about her.'

'What a surprise! This is all very frustrating.'

'Without meaning to sound facetious—' said Jen, looping her arm through Claire's.

'A recurring theme with you,' Claire interrupted.

'—can I treat you to a scone?'

Chapter 34

18th century, Edinburgh

Pringle cast an anxious glance across the crowd gathering on the snowy banks of Duddingston Loch. A fresh snowfall had given the surrounding countryside a crisp sharpness, the trees with their spindly branches reaching for the blue sky. There were many faces he recognised from the Edinburgh literati: Creech, the publisher, stood with Mr Burns and Mrs McElhose. Mr Foote was there with Smellie, his bad-tempered assistant. The Reverend Robert Walker's family were all there; Magdalen gave him a friendly wave. She was clutching that cursed doll in her other hand. Mr Smith was hugging himself in the bitter cold of the day, and the Smeaton twins were there too with

225

their tartan-clad pug. Even Squirrel was there, hurtling around the ice, showing off to the crowd.

But no Katherine, and no Mr Hume. Where on earth were they?

Pringle glanced around anxiously. His hands were sweaty, despite the freezing temperatures. Katherine had been with him through every challenge and outing over the last few weeks; it was inconceivable that she wouldn't be here today. He realised he had come to rely on her presence. If he achieved his goal and succeeded in being accepted into the Edinburgh Skating Club, he would be invited to attend the annual club dinner that very night, and dine on sheeps' heads and trotters and raise a glass whilst wearing the silver medal, the words *Ocior Euro* etched into its cold, heavy surface.

But none of this would happen, he thought to himself, without Katherine there too. She was his amulet, his four-leafed clover, his lucky charm.

Around him, skaters were warming up and demonstrating their skills. It was impressive and intimidating. He felt a lurch in his stomach. The Reverend Robert Walker was there, skating with his usual flair. And now the other gentlemen members of the club began to skate together, slowly and in unison. It was a graceful sight. They gathered first to create a harmonious and smooth 'worm', also known as the 'screw'. Their skates cut and scored the ice in wonderful circular patterns as they effortlessly snaked closely together following the leader. Next, balls were placed at measured distances and each member skated around the ball in a perfect circle, corresponding exactly in shape, direction and timing with his opposite number, culminating in a complex weaving motion of bodies, close but never touching. Last came the most stunning spectacle of all: the Wild Goose. Two circles of skaters throwing themselves forward on to one foot, one line on their right foot moving in one direction, the other on their left foot going the other way. The two groups continued skating, the circles getting smaller and smaller, until the skaters met in the middle. It was a triumph!

The crowd was delighted by the sight, and cries of approval, wonder and awe were followed by applause and the throwing of hats into the air. But then came the moment Pringle had been awaiting with breath that was most certainly bated. It was time for his skills test. He felt slightly sick, and once more glanced around the crowd. At last a carriage pulled up close to the loch, and Pringle watched as Katherine clambered out of it with Foxey tucked under her arm. She pushed her way through the crowd to a place where she could see Pringle and gave him a small wave. Relieved, Pringle asked the judges for a moment to have a quiet word with her, and skated over to where she was standing.

'You're here at last,' he said. 'Where have you been?'

'Forgive me, Francis.' Katherine was clearly not quite herself. She seemed tense, and looked pinched. Foxey, however, was thrilled to see Pringle and wagged his brush of a tail, wriggling and whimpering and trying to lick his gloved hands.

'What is wrong, Katherine?' Pringle asked, stroking the little dog in her arms. 'Are you quite well?'

'Oh, it is nothing,' she said, with a wave of her hand. 'David is a little under the weather. He has taken to his bed. He is most distressed not to be here to offer his support, dear Francis. He so wanted to come.'

'But you should be with him,' said Pringle. 'Don't concern yourself with this. Go back to your brother, and I will come directly.'

'No, no.' She was defiant. 'I promised you. And he was adamant that I must come and pass on his very best wishes to you.'

Pringle gazed into Katherine's eyes. He sensed that there was something she would not allow herself to say.

'Now, go, and show us all what you are made of,' she said, lifting her chin. 'This, dear Francis, is what we have been waiting for. It's your moment of triumph!'

Pringle nodded, took a deep breath, and set off once more to the centre of the ice.

The trial began with simple moves. He had to complete two circles first on one foot, then on the other. The crowd applauded as he managed this with ease.

Next came the jumps. When a hat was placed in the middle of the ice, Pringle glanced over to Squirrel. The little wretch stuck out his tongue and waggled his hands above his head. Katherine, though, was smiling broadly at him – willing him to succeed. Even Foxey seemed to be grinning.

'When you are ready, Mr Pringle,' said the Reverend Robert Walker.

Pringle took a deep breath and took off towards the hat. His speed was good, and he remembered to bend his knees deeply and use his arms to propel himself. He leapt into the air and landed smoothly to a cheer from the crowd. He swept round past beaming faces back to his starting position ready for hat number two.

Once again, Pringle took a deep breath. From somewhere in the crowd, he heard a shout. 'Go on, Feartie Face, ye can do it!'

There was no need to look where that voice came from. He knew Squirrel was taunting him with the best of intentions. He took off at a faster pace and once again leapt and landed to a tremendous cheer. He saw Katherine celebrating as he passed. The crowd were thoroughly enjoying the test.

And now there was only one challenge left between him and that coveted silver medal. The third hat was placed on the pile and Pringle took a final deep breath. The noise from the crowd dipped as everyone waited and watched. The only sounds now were the distant cry of a bird, or a shout from someone far away. Pringle allowed himself to enjoy the moment. He quickly glanced around at the expectant crowd and was just about to set off once more when for a fleeting second he thought he glimpsed a familiar face. He frowned, but set off anyway, building speed and momentum. As he approached the stack of hats, he couldn't help but look once more at the crowd, and realised just as he leapt high into the air that the face he had been so struck by was someone he knew extremely well. It was his son.

He landed elegantly, without a stumble, to rapturous applause. The other members of the Skating Club gathered around him to pump his hand and slap him on the back.

His eyes searched the crowd once more, just to be sure, but his son must have gone. He didn't really need confirmation; he knew deep down it had been Adam. He could not focus on the moments that followed as he stood alone on the ice, waiting. He was vaguely aware of a speedy ballot by the members of the Edinburgh Skating Club, then the counting of votes as everyone waited. There was a hush as the Reverend Robert Walker stepped forward to make the announcement, and finally there were raucous cheers from the crowd as the silver medal Pringle had so coveted was placed around his neck. He didn't see Squirrel fling his cap into the air and whistle through his fingers so loudly that a furious Mr Smith was rendered temporarily deaf. He didn't see Mr Foote and Smellie hug in delight. He didn't see Katherine lift up Foxey in celebration, tears flowing down her cheeks. He didn't see any of it.

Instead of joy, Pringle felt utterly wretched.

Chapter 35

21st century, Edinburgh

'Will you still talk to me?' said Jen, scooping a spoonful of fried rice on to her plate from the plastic container.

'What?' said Claire, who was decanting the take-away from the flimsy plastic bag on to her coffee table.

'When you're rich and famous.'

'Oh yeah,' said Claire. 'That'll be the day. But yes, I will still talk to you. From the lofty height of my pedestal.'

She took off the last container lid and then sat down to serve herself and Jen. They were in Claire's flat and the television was on, but the sound was muted. They were waiting to see Claire on the local evening news.

'Why you? If you don't mind my asking?' said Jen, her mouth full as she pointed her fork towards the television. A tiny bit of sauce dribbled down her chin.

'They asked. The National Gallery didn't want to at this stage, and Brian said I should perhaps do it since it was me who started it in the first place,' said Claire. 'He said it would raise the profile of the department. In a good way.' She picked up a paper napkin and dabbed Jen's chin for her.

Jen put her plate down and took the napkin to finish the job. 'Thanks,' she said.

'Oh, look. Here goes.' Claire reached over to unmute the television. 'Oh God, I look ancient!'

'Not at all,' said Jen. 'You look distinguished.'

Wearing the smartest outfit she could muster from her limited wardrobe, she was standing slightly side-on in front of the newly restored painting from the Black and White corridor, looking at an invisible person who was feeding her questions.

'Well, the discovery that *this* painting is in fact of the Reverend Robert Walker suggests that the one hanging in the National Gallery is by someone else entirely. This painting is in the more traditional style we recognise as that of a Raeburn portrait: the Reverend Robert Walker is in his ministerial robes, and was most likely painted at Raeburn's studio in the New Town. The idea that Raeburn would choose to paint an action shot of such a distinguished gentleman makes the skating portrait even more unlikely to be his work.'

'So, who painted the Skating Minister? That's the question everyone is asking,' said the voice off screen.

'Well, let's address who the skater is first of all, as it may be a surprise to many,' said the onscreen Claire. 'The so-called "skating minister" may not be Robert Walker at all, but another member of the Edinburgh Skating Club. Early research suggests it could be Mr Francis Pringle, something of a celebrity of the time, who was a good friend of several Enlightenment figures, including philosopher and writer David Hume.'

'Okay, so going back to who actually painted him,' pressed the invisible presenter, 'it's been previously suggested that the skater is in fact by Frenchman Henri-Pierre Danloux. What are your thoughts on that, Dr Sharp?'

'I'm going to throw a controversial spanner in the works here,' said Claire with a smile, 'and say that I don't think that to be the case.' She paused. 'My research has led me to believe that this painting is in fact by a woman. Possibly even David Hume's sister, Katherine. My colleague from the Scottish History faculty here at the university and I are now actively looking for information about this fascinating woman's life.'

Jen gave Claire a nudge.

The offscreen voice interjected, 'That is quite a controversial statement, Dr Sharp, for such an iconic image.'

'Well, I believe we need to explore the fact that women were painting, writing, thinking – in fact, actually existing at that time. History has, to use a very current and apt expression, "airbrushed out" their contribution for too long, and in particular they have been simply removed from the Enlightenment movement. It's really time we set the record straight and recognised the invaluable contribution women have made to the progression of society.'

The camera pulled back and the scene switched back to the studio. Claire reached for the remote control and clicked off the TV.

Wide-eyed, Jen turned to look at her. 'Bravo, Claire. Bravo!'

'Really?' said Claire. 'Do you think I went too far?'

'Absolutely not,' said Jen. 'But . . .'

'Oh, here it comes.'

'You want me to be completely honest, don't you?'

'Yes.' Claire put her plate back on the table. 'Of course I do.'

'Well, I thought it was bold and beautiful, but others out there might be a teensy bit shocked.'

'Well, okay, but that's all right.'

Just as she said this, Claire's phone began buzzing

on the kitchen table. She jumped up to check it. It buzzed again and again.

'Texts,' she said. 'Lots and lots of text messages.'

'Who from?'

'Er, mainly from my students,' said Claire, scrolling through them. 'Mmm . . . all very positive . . . I think.' The phone continued to buzz. Then it began to ring.

'Oh, turn the damn thing off. At least till we've finished our dinner,' said Jen. 'It's so annoying.'

Claire pressed the side button on the phone and the screen went blank. 'There,' she said. 'That's better. Right. Well, that was all good.' But she was frowning. 'Funny so many people texting me.'

'Well, that's the way things go these days,' said Jen. 'It's how *they* all communicate.'

'It's given me a bit of a weird feeling,' Claire said, continuing to stand by the kitchen table. She absent-mindedly chewed a finger nail.

'Come and eat,' said Jen, 'before I polish the whole lot off.'

Claire wandered back over and sat down beside Jen. She swallowed a forkful of lemon chicken, and they ate in silence for a while, both deep in thought.

'Did you discuss what you were going to say with Brian before the interview?' Jen asked.

Claire shook her head and swallowed. 'No, I didn't feel I needed to. They were asking my opinion, after all.

I thought I would just say what I was feeling.'

Jen nodded. She tipped the last of the rice on to her plate. 'Well, you certainly told the world how you felt.'

'What's that supposed to mean?'

'I think the technical term is "going off on one",' said Jen. 'I could practically see the steam coming out of your ears.'

'What do you mean? Was I really that bad?' Claire dropped her fork on to her plate with a clatter. 'Oh God.' She began wafting her jumper. 'I think I'm having a hot flush.'

'No, no, I'm teasing,' said Jen, waving her hand. 'You were superb. Stick your head out the window; that always helps me.'

'I think I'll open the wine. That'll *really* help,' said Claire.

She was just standing up when the main door buzzer sounded, making her jump. 'For God's sake,' she snapped. 'Who could that be?'

She went through to the hallway and picked up the intercom phone. 'Hello?'

'Dr Sharp? It's Peter. Can I come up?' He was shouting, for some reason, and sounded a bit excited. 'I tried to ring but your phone was off. That interview you did. You've gone viral!'

Chapter 36

18th century, Edinburgh

Alison Cockburn sat alone in her flat. She had managed to escape from Duddingston as quickly as possible. Once home, she had set and lit the fire and kitchen range and managed, in a very short space of time, to make the house feel lived in. Panic had driven her to do this at speed, and now, as she sat in her parlour awaiting the arrival of her son, she had begun to feel something quite unexpected. She felt an overwhelming sense of shame. She had no time to dwell on it, however, as there was the sound of the key in the lock and the door opened. There were footsteps in the hall, and then her son came into the parlour.

'Adam!' She stood up, attempting to keep her voice

light in spite of the sudden urge to cry. 'What a surprise!'

'Mother,' he said, and lightly kissed her cheek. 'You're here. I came by earlier but there was no sign of you. Have you been out?'

'Yes,' she said. 'Just for a walk. I'm sorry I wasn't here when you arrived. I had no idea you were coming.'

Adam frowned. 'Well, I did write,' he said, his voice flat and quiet. 'But you never replied.'

Alison glanced over to the pile of unopened letters sitting on the table. 'I'm so sorry, dear, I've been a little busy,' she said.

'I arrived last night, Mother.' Adam's eyebrows were still knitted together. 'There was no sign of life in the house, and the fires hadn't been lit for some time.' He stared at her. 'Where have you been?'

Alison sighed. Where to begin?

'Where did you go?' she asked brightly instead. 'Did you stay here?'

'No. I dined with friends, and stayed the night with Thomas. We had much catching up to do.'

Alison nodded. 'I see. And are you here on a long visit?'

'Yes,' he said. 'If you don't mind, I thought I might stay here for a few weeks, perhaps until the middle of January.'

There was a long pause. Adam was the first to speak again.

'You don't seem terribly pleased to see me, Mother. And where were you last night?'

'I was visiting friends,' said Alison. 'Miss Hume and I were staying in Cramond.' Could he tell she was lying? She thought he probably could.

Adam nodded. He seemed satisfied for the present and took off his hat before sitting down near the fire.

'Goodness, it's cold,' he said. 'I have just come from Duddingston.'

'Oh, really?' said Alison. 'And what, pray, were you doing there? Skating?' She smiled, and then wished she'd kept her mouth closed.

'No, Thomas and I were taking some air,' he said. 'But there were many skaters on the loch. In fact, there was a performance of sorts by a skating club. It was very impressive. And some gentleman was jumping over hats.'

Alison nodded. 'Interesting. Well, now,' she said, standing up, 'will you take some tea? I'm without a housemaid at the moment, but I can make you some myself.'

'Thank you. No housemaid?' said Adam, tutting. 'Dear me, Mother.'

She shrugged and smiled.

'And what of the Humes?' he continued. 'How are they both?'

Alison had forgotten all about the Humes. She wondered what on earth Katherine must have thought.

As soon as she had spotted Adam, she had felt that she was betraying her son. It was truly horrifying. The world of Francis Pringle had come crashing down and she was Alison Cockburn once more. Hiding from the crowd, she had whipped off her skates and run as fast as she could back towards the Royal Mile, where she had rushed to the flat in James Court. There, she had stripped off as quickly as possible and dressed herself again as Alison Cockburn before heading at speed to her own flat in Crichton Street. Everything felt so strange and different. Walking in petticoats and a long skirt once more was billowy and uncomfortable; indeed, she had tripped a few times. But, mercifully, she garnered no interest. Nobody looked her way. Gone was congenial, sociable and handsome Mr Pringle. Invisible Mrs Cockburn had returned.

She considered her friend Mr Hume, at home and unwell, and her stomach lurched. 'I believe Mr Hume is not keeping too well,' she said, 'but Katherine is in good health.'

'So I saw,' said Adam. 'It is strange that you say she was with you in Cramond, when I saw her at Duddingston too. She had Foxey with her.'

'Oh, really?' said Alison. She had her back to Adam, and she closed her eyes. Her head was throbbing, her throat dry.

'Strange that she was there and you didn't know, when you had apparently been to Cramond together.

You two are usually thick as thieves. And she was there despite her brother's being unwell? How peculiar! She seemed quite engrossed in the skating, or certainly in the man who was skating at the time. I did call to her, but she didn't hear me, so intent was she on the skater.'

'Indeed?' said Alison. She looked around the pantry and realised there was no food in the house, nothing for them to have for supper. Her mind was racing with panic.

'What is going on, Mother?' Adam persisted. 'You are being very mysterious. I should tell you that when I found you weren't here last night, I asked a messenger who happened to be on the stairs where you might be. He said he had heard you were in Glasgow, staying with me.'

Alison felt a rush to her head and creeping black spots spread across her eyes. She reached for the table, but then her legs gave way beneath her, and she collapsed to the floor.

When Alison opened her eyes, she was lying on her bed and her son was staring at her, his face all concern and anxiety.

'Mother!' he exclaimed. 'Thank goodness you have awoken. You have been taken quite unwell. You were talking wildly, but not making any sense. I shall go and call for a physician.'

Alison grabbed her son's arm. 'No, please. Don't do that,' she said. Then she sighed. 'I need to explain, to tell you . . . where I've been. What has happened. I cannot lie to my flesh and blood; I must tell you about Francis Pringle.'

An hour later, her son was on his way back to Glasgow.

Chapter 37

21st century, Edinburgh

'What's this all about?' said Claire, leaning over the banister. She could just see Peter's legs as he wound his way up to her flat on the top floor.

'That interview. It's being shared on social media, right now,' he said, a little out of breath. He arrived at the top and held out his phone. 'Here, just look at the number of times it's been shared already!'

Claire glanced at the screen. 'I don't even know what I'm looking at.'

'Four hundred times. And that's just on one platform,' said Peter. 'There's a clip doing the rounds on Twitter too. And someone's made a gif out of you already and stuck it on the head of the Skating Minister painting. You were only on the air twenty minutes ago. This is massive! You're a celebrity!' Peter was still scrolling through his phone when the door on the opposite side of the stairwell opened and a man in a shabby suit came out. He was about to head down the steps when he noticed Claire.

'I saw you on the gogglebox, Claire,' he said. 'I had no idea you were a raving feminist.' And then, before she could think of something even vaguely appropriate to retort, he scuttled out of sight, like a rabbit down a hole.

Claire stared after him, her mouth open in shock. 'I've spoken two words to that man in ten years and he now sees fit to call me a raving feminist,' she said.

'That might be the kindest thing you'll hear for a bit,' said Peter, his eyes still glued to the little screen in front of him.

Claire turned and marched into the flat with Peter. 'Feminist? What's he talking about?' she muttered. 'It's not feminism to demand historical equity. It's not feminism to set the record straight. It's justice. And hang on a minute, what do you mean *kindest thing I'll hear for a bit*?' She slammed the door behind them and swung round to face Peter. 'Is this because I didn't announce to the world that it was a painting by your hero, *the precious Henri-Pierre bloody Danloux*?'

'No, no, not at all. I don't disagree with what you

said. I found it very interesting.' He frowned. 'It's just that you've upset two major factions of our society. I'm not talking academics here; I mean nationalists and misogynists.'

'What? That's ridiculous. It's a painting, for goodness' sake. I was just telling the truth.'

'Check your phone,' said Jen, handing it over.

Claire turned it on and waited for it to fire up. Her mind was racing. Had her comments been so controversial? She realised her hands were shaking.

The phone began to buzz almost instantly with text messages and emails. Then a voicemail notification appeared. She tentatively lifted the phone to her ear. It was Brian.

'It's my boss,' she said, putting it on speaker. 'Oh God, what's he going to say about all this?'

Brian's voice blared out of the phone. ' . . . I need to speak to the actual Claire Sharp and not your voicemail. I've had the National Gallery on the phone and it's safe to say they're pretty disgruntled by your interview, and I am too. What were you thinking? A well-respected art historian, and your comments were fanciful and instinct-driven at best, feminist propaganda bullshit-based or some sort of personal vendetta at worst!' There was a brief pause as Brian caught his breath. He sounded incandescent with rage. 'You sounded like an amateur sleuth, Claire, not an academic. I can't believe you didn't run this one by me first. The gallery want to distance themselves from it, which is not great for the university. Or for you.' The phone clicked off.

Claire stood still, quite stunned. 'I didn't even need to put that on speaker, he was shouting so loud.' She shook her head. 'What was that all about?'

'What a snake,' said Jen. 'I never liked that man.'

'He was leaping for joy over the Black and White corridor Raeburn being the real Robert Walker. He was calling my research "genius" and "ground-breaking". Now I'm an amateur spouting feminist bullshit?'

'He'll have gauged the gallery's reaction and reset his own to match. That man bends with the wind,' said Jen bitterly. 'Weak. The worst sort.'

'Some posts here are implying the university have launched an attack on an iconic Scottish image,' Peter reported, eyes still fixed on his phone, 'and it's therefore an attack on Scotland.'

'*What?* That's a bit of a stretch, isn't it?' said Jen, rolling her eyes.

'But I'm not saying it's not a Scotsman skating!' Claire tried not to shout. 'I'm not even saying it's been painted by a Frenchman. I'm *suggesting* it's the work of a Scottish *woman*. Why is that so offensive? And I wasn't speaking on behalf of the university.'

'It will blow over,' said Peter, trying to sound reassuring. 'Er, do you have a Twitter account?'

'Yes, now you come to mention it, I do,' said Claire. 'But I don't really use it.'

'Well, I suggest you don't look at it . . . ah, yes, I've found you. No, really don't look at it.'

'So what am I supposed to do, then? Make some sort of statement retracting everything?'

'God, no,' said Jen. 'Today's news, tomorrow's chip paper.'

'If I were you, I'd lie low for a day or two.' Peter was still attempting to sound reassuring.

'Well, I'm not going to lie low,' said Claire. 'No way. Why should I? I've not mugged a granny or robbed a bank. It's all gone completely over the top. And I have a job to do.'

By the time Jen and Peter had left, a kind of melancholy had swept over Claire. Jen had clasped her hand at the front door and reminded her of the Rudyard Kipling poem, 'If'. Something about keeping her head when everyone else had lost theirs and was blaming her. Jen was worried about her, she could tell.

Now she sat slumped on the sofa, a cold cup of tea beside her. From time to time she switched on her phone and scrolled through the text messages and emails that were appearing as if on a conveyor belt of doom. They were endless. There were several missed calls too, all redirected into her voicemail. She dared not listen.

Most messages, she told herself, were positive. There was solidarity at this shout out for forgotten women. But many were downright unpleasant. And some . . . some were simply too vile to contemplate.

Claire rewatched the clip of herself, and, cringing at her own words, she felt her morale and self-belief slipping. The Twitter account she had forgotten she even had had in just over two hours become a toxic cesspit of misogyny and abuse. She tried to shut down the damn thing but even that seemed beyond her. Emailers jostling for position in her inbox ranged from newspapers begging for interviews, no doubt with some sort of Schadenfreude in mind, to colleagues and fellow art historians expressing surprise, indignation and downright horror at her statement on the news.

She'd had enough. She switched her phone and laptop off and put them in the cupboard, then ran herself a deep bath. As she slipped into the scalding water she wondered if this was all her career had come to: a half-baked rant on the evening news. It was likely that resignation would be her only option. Clawing back her reputation would take some sort of miracle.

She peered through the veil of misery in her mind and began slowly to sift and sort everything she and Jen had discussed during this whole business. The word she kept coming back to was 'obsessive'. It had been used by Jen to describe the artist in her approach to her subject: not a tangible thing, like a brush stroke, but something Jen had felt had emanated from the canvas, and she was absolutely correct. Suddenly Claire sat up in the bath. She understood.

Whoever painted the skating minister wasn't painting him for money, or for a commission. She was painting for love. Pure, unfaltering love.

Chapter 38

18th century, Edinburgh

It was, concluded Alison Cockburn, as if none of it had ever happened. It was Christmas Eve, and she had never felt quite so alone. She stopped for a moment in the High Street and peered up at the gloomy sky. Snow was falling heavily, in large, feathery flakes that settled on the rooftops, the cobbles and now on her eyelashes.

It was so cold that the streets were quiet and eerily empty. Christmas was a time for family and friends, for reunion and celebration, but this year, Alison conceded, she had no one. Once again dressed in long skirts that twisted uncomfortably around her thighs, or trailed in the snow, Alison raised the hood on her cape and wrapped her clasped hands tightly together, pulling her scarf to her nose. Nobody called out to her; nobody wished her a good day as she traversed the street, avoiding the nastiness mushed into the freshly fallen snow as she made her way to James Court. She had left many of her belongings there and it was time to begin to piece her life, her old life, back together again.

She had remained in hiding for several days after Adam had left, too ashamed to show her face. Her son had been incandescent with horror at the actions of his mother. He was disgusted with her, mortified, and could not bear to look at her or think of what she had done. Her behaviour had been perfidious, reckless and sinful; she had made a mockery of the fine community of Edinburgh, he had said. She had hoodwinked good people; a minister too, for heaven's sake. Her behaviour was deplorable. He did not wish to discuss it, or to think on it further, and so had fled back to Glasgow. It had been a most unpleasant scene and had left Alison distraught.

The shame of it all had crept over her and remained there like a rash. She wanted to wash it all away. She had wondered too how Mr Hume was. And Katherine. Oh, Katherine! Even thinking about her made Alison's heart ache. Alison had left her dear friend, abandoned her without word or explanation after scolding her for coming late to the loch. Had Katherine seen her running away? Had she spotted Adam? It was too painful to think of. She had attempted to write, but every time she had tried to put pen to paper the words were woefully inadequate.

She imagined that the Edinburgh Skating Club, so thrilled with their new addition, had been left scratching their heads at the sudden and quite unexplained disappearance of the triumphant Pringle. At dinner that night they would have raised their glasses to toast the empty seat of their newest member, baffled by his vanishing act. Alison could feel the medal, heavy on her skin under her shift. She had told herself that she didn't want to leave it lying around to betray her, but the truth was she couldn't bear to take it off.

Lunches arranged, meetings planned, all had been abandoned. Her dreams of being published dashed. William Creech was still awaiting Pringle's visit to his luckenbooth: a visit that would never occur now. But it was the friendships that had gone without a trace, that left a sense of abandonment, a desperation, washing over Alison.

As she walked down the narrow close towards the houses at the end, she could see the silhouette of a man standing in the courtyard beyond, holding a cane. It was Samuel Foote.

He turned to look at her as she approached. His normally joyful, funny face looked quite different. He stared at Alison with a terrible anguish.

'My dear,' he said, 'I have been coming here every day in the hope that I would see you eventually. You see, I don't know where you, as you, live.'

'Good day, Mr Foote,' said Alison, trying to make her voice sound as cheerful as possible. 'Will you come inside? It is bitterly cold, and there are some items I need to collect.'

They walked towards the front door and Alison produced a key. Mr Foote reached out a gloved hand to hold hers, and felt it trembling.

'How small your hands are, my dear,' said Mr Foote. 'I had not noticed before.'

Alison smiled and shrugged, and then unlocked the door.

Upstairs, inside the flat, there was something of a mess on the floor. Skates had been thrown down, as had a hat, breeches and stockings. Unapologetic, Alison began picking up, sorting and tidying. She placed Pringle's clothes in a pile.

'It's just as well you're here, actually,' she said. 'I won't be needing these any more. We can arrange for Smellie, or some messenger boy, to have them collected and returned to your theatrical costume chest.'

'Mrs Cockburn, I came on purpose to find you,' said Foote quietly.

'Indeed.' Alison continued to arrange the clothing.

'My dear, Mr Hume has died.'

Alison dropped the coat she was holding. She let out a gasp and fell to her knees, her head in her hands. 'No,' she said. 'No, no, say it isn't so.' She pulled off her hood and cap and grasped at her hair. Then she looked up into the anxious face of Foote, waiting for him to tell her he had made a mistake, that his remark was an ill-judged prank, but instead he knelt down beside her. She began to sob softly on to his shoulder, and he put his arm around her.

'I am so sorry,' he said. He reached into his pocket and withdrew a handkerchief which he handed to Alison, who was rocking forwards and back. She heard someone wailing before she realised it was her own self.

'Oh, dear Lord,' she said, pressing the handkerchief to her eyes. 'Oh, no. My poor, poor Katherine. When did he die?'

'It was some days ago, dear one,' said Foote. 'The funeral was this morning.'

Alison stared at him, horrified. 'How can it be? Why did no one tell me?'

'I have been trying to find a way to contact you,' said Foote. 'But Katherine wouldn't hear of it. She has taken it all so badly. She insisted that you shouldn't be told. She was very upset by your . . . ' he paused, searching for the word, 'disappearance.'

Alison, quite wild with an overwhelming grief, stumbled to her feet, and without another word to a startled Mr Foote she staggered out of the flat. She heard him shout after her as she ran down the stairwell, but she didn't stop. Outside, slithering over the snow, she hurtled back up the close and down on to the Lawnmarket. She ran down the High Street, hoisting up her skirts, sliding and stumbling in the snow that had piled up by the road but caring not. Her tears flowed down her cheeks as she went. She turned on to North Bridge and continued to run, her heart pounding in her chest, the falling snow now driving into her eyes. She did not stop running until she arrived at the Humes' house, where she pounded her freezing fist on the door. It was opened by Peggy, who gawped at the sight of a bedraggled and tear-stained Mrs Alison Cockburn.

'Where is Miss Hume?' Alison cried. 'I must see her.'

'Miss Hume does not wish to be disturbed, madam,' said Peggy piously. Alison pushed past her and ran to the parlour, but there was no one there.

'Katherine?' she called, checking every room.

At last Katherine appeared on the staircase. She looked quite appalled when she saw Alison. She was wearing black from head to toe, and her face was pale. She stared down at her friend with a mixture of shame and horror.

'Katherine, why did you not tell me?' Alison looked up. 'My dearest?' Tears were once more flowing down her face.

'I can't see you,' said Katherine, turning to go back up the stairs. 'Please leave. I want no more of this. I wish we had never dreamt up such a disgraceful scheme.'

'But it's over now,' said Alison. 'See, dear friend. I am back to myself! And David is no longer here. How could you not tell me about the funeral? I did not pay my respects.'

Peggy was loitering in the hall.

Katherine turned back and wiped tears from her face. 'Tell you?' She spat the words. 'You who fled from Duddingston? Leaving me? I was mortified. You abandoned me.'

'But I had to,' said Alison. 'You don't understand. I had no choice.'

'Imagine what everyone thought about it . . . about us? And how it looked when you vanished.'

'Us? I don't know what you mean, Katherine.'

'Everyone thought we had an understanding. And when you ran off, people talked! Some said they saw you scurry away like a child who has done something wrong. Scandalous rumours were rife, and then you simply disappeared without a single word. You didn't explain or seek to tell me why. What was I to think? What was everyone to think?'

Alison stared at her friend, trying to understand what she was saying. 'Wait,' she said slowly. 'You say . . . an understanding? You mean an *engagement*?'

'And you weren't even there at David's funeral, his own cousin!' Katherine was rubbing her forehead as if it ached.

Alison took in the words and stood quite still. They were both perfectly silent, the sonorous ticking of the clock in the hall the only sound between them.

'Katherine, you are confused,' Alison said, at last. 'I am not actually David's cousin, am I? My son returned.' Her voice was quiet and calm. 'Adam knows about our little jest. He knows all about Francis Pringle and he is furious. I had to end it then. But it had to come to an end at some point; you must have foreseen that?'

For a moment there was a look in Katherine's eyes so full of anguish and confusion that Alison could hardly bear to look at her.

'All I've heard since you disappeared is where is Pringle? Why has he left? Oh, the tumult you have unleashed in my heart.' Tears were streaming down Katherine's face. Alison took a step towards her, her hands outreached to offer comfort, but Katherine stepped back, her expression appalled. 'I wish we'd never done it,' she said angrily. 'That we'd never created that foolish and stupid man.'

Alison took a deep breath. 'Katherine, I am so, so sorry,' she said. 'We didn't know. We couldn't have known where any of this would lead. And you are grieving for your brother too, my dearest. Please let me comfort you.'

Now Katherine began to sob, great heaving gulps of despair. She put her hand to her mouth and tried to steady herself.

'My heart is breaking.' The words were barely audible as tears ran like rivers down her face. 'I loved my brother dearly, but I adored Francis Pringle. I loved him as I have never loved anyone before. And now they are both gone!'

Then she turned and ran back up the stairs and slammed a door. Her sobs could be heard from some distant room, muffled by a pillow.

Alison was left, bewildered, on the stairs. Peggy shifted awkwardly in the hall below. Aware of the housekeeper's eyes on her, Alison tried to stem her own tears with shaking hands, and walked back down to the front door and out into the street.

Chapter 39

21st century, Edinburgh

When Claire awoke the next morning, she felt a new sense of determination. It was Saturday, and as far as she was concerned she didn't have to speak to Brian until at least Monday morning. That gave her the weekend to work out how she was going to proceed. She also felt that it would be wise to take the bull by the horns, turn on her computer, gauge the level of hatred towards her and let that inform her next step – which might involve putting on dark glasses and a baseball cap to do her weekly shop. Or perhaps, just perhaps, the average person on the street didn't give two hoots about a random painting in the hallowed corridors of the National Gallery and she could have two days of peace and quiet as she moved around the city.

What she wasn't going to do was wallow in self-pity or self-indulgent wailing about how her words had been taken out of context or misunderstood. They hadn't and she had meant every damn one of them. One way or another she was ready for the fight. What had she once boasted to Peter's group in the Beehive during a boozy tutorial? That within reason she could convincingly argue attribution of any painting? Well, now she would put that to the test.

She retrieved her phone and her laptop from the cupboard, made herself a large mug of coffee and sat down to discover the worst. The majority of what she had been sent certainly wasn't for the faint-hearted. She cursed her email address being so readily available on the university web page. She was so easy to access! In amongst the solidarity, which was nice, were mockery and some questioning of her academic competence, which she found patronising and irritating, but the worst messages were sinister and even threatening. However, the delete button was liberating, and the particularly vile ones were put into a folder marked 'FAO POLICE'. She reflected that she had had no idea there were so many Raeburn fanatics around the world, or for that matter nationalists so empowered by an image painted over two hundred years earlier.

And Brian could bloody well wait too. He had followed up his phone message with an email that was bordering on hysterical. It made her grin to think of him typing it, fingers flying, smoke rising from the keyboard. He could sweat. She was under no obligation to say anything at this stage. She was relieved that her sense of humour had returned, and she could see the funny side of it all.

But then, in amongst the midden of emails, something caught her eye.

It was from an Andrew Ross, with the subject heading *Katherine Hume*. She clicked on it.

Dear Dr Sharp,

My mother and I saw you on the news last night and I'm emailing you on her behalf. I wondered if it might be possible to talk to you. We have some information about the late Katherine Hume, sister of David Hume, that might be of interest to you in your research.

It would be best to meet you in person. Perhaps you could call me on the number below to arrange. We live in Eskbank – would it be a problem to come out to us?

With very best wishes,

Andrew Ross (and Mrs Margaret Ross)

Claire picked up her phone and dialled the number at the bottom of the email. She braced herself in case this was an elaborate excuse to hurl abuse at her. Well, one way or another she would quickly find out.

'Hello?'

'Is that Mr Ross?'

'Yes.' The man sounded quite old.

'Mr Ross, this is Claire Sharp. You emailed me on behalf of your mother.'

'Ah yes,' the man said. 'How marvellous that you phoned me back. And so quickly, too.'

'You have some information on Katherine Hume?' Claire asked tentatively.

'We do indeed,' said Andrew. 'We have something we want to show you.' Then he began to laugh, not in a cruel way but in a rather light-hearted manner. He sounded quite endearing, and Claire found it refreshing after all the hostile emails she'd had to endure.

'It sounds intriguing,' she said. 'Can you tell me any more over the phone?'

'Well, you see, it's quite incredible that we should have seen your interview on the television, Dr Sharp,' said Andrew, 'because my mother and I are direct descendants of the Hume family and the custodians, as it were, of Katherine Hume's diaries.'

Chapter 40

'What a turn up for the books,' said Jen as she and Claire drove out of Edinburgh on the city's bypass. 'Katherine Hume's actual diaries. It's wonderful!'

'I know. Andrew Ross didn't say much on the phone, just that we needed to see them for ourselves.'

'Well, let's hope he's not some sort of raving fantasist.'

'After having spent the morning reading the emails in my inbox, nothing would surprise me,' said Claire with a sigh.

They turned off the vehicle-choked dual carriageway and headed over the River Esk towards the semi-rural surroundings of Eskbank. 'Even if this all comes to nothing, it's a relief to get out of the city,' Claire commented.

Jen nodded. 'Absolutely. You can breathe out here. And it's good to get a sense of perspective, isn't it?'

Claire smiled. 'You mean the world doesn't revolve around art and academia?'

Jen laughed. 'God, I hope not!'

'Why is it that sometimes life feels like such a battlefield?'

'It's a stark reminder we must put on our invisible armour along with our smalls in the morning.'

'So true,' said Claire.

'It's not all bad. And what gets you through it, my dear, is humour, and—'

'Wine!'

Jen laughed. 'Yes! And a good pal who'll drive you wherever you need to go.'

They turned down a wide street of neat 1960s bungalows and began to check the house numbers.

'The next one on the left, I think,' said Claire, and they turned into the driveway. The garden was immaculate, the lawn trimmed, the edges sharp.

'It doesn't look like the house of a maniac, I must say,' said Jen, peering out of the windscreen.

'Or he's a very neat and tidy one,' said Claire.

Andrew Ross was already at the front door. He gave them a cheerful wave as they approached. He was not quite as old as Claire had thought. Probably in his seventies, he wore a red sweater and a large grin.

'Dr Sharp, so good of you to come,' he said. 'Do come inside.'

'Just call me Claire. And this is my good friend, historian and fellow academic Jen Brodie.'

'Just call me Professor,' said Jen with a smile.

'Well, I am very honoured,' said Andrew Ross, and shook hands with them both. He ushered them into the house, which was dated in its decor but as immaculate as the garden, and took them through to a conservatory at the back, where an elderly woman sat in a chair gazing out at the vista of neat pathways and tidy shrubs.

'Mother?' said Andrew in a loud voice, moving closer to her. 'The lady from the TV is here. The one researching Katherine Hume. She's brought her friend, who's a history professor.' He nodded at Jen, clearly rather impressed. Jen gave him a wink.

The woman looked up at him and then at Claire and Jen. She was slender, with long white hair swept back into a low ponytail and a bony frame encased in a pink cardigan. At first she didn't respond, but all of a sudden her face lit up with energy.

'Hello, Mrs Ross,' said Claire. 'I'm Claire Sharp and this is Jen Brodie.'

'She had a stroke a few months back,' said Andrew. 'Lost her speech. She's pretty deaf too now. And as you can see, she's lost the use of her right hand.' Sure enough, the woman cradled her right hand and shifted it from time to time with her left.

'Do take a seat,' Andrew went on. 'I'll make us some tea.' He left the room, and Claire and Jen sat down on two wicker armchairs. There was an uncomfortable silence, punctuated by the steady tick-tock of a clock somewhere in the house. They glanced at each other, and the woman continued to smile.

'So, I believe you know something about Katherine Hume?' said Claire loudly.

Mrs Ross nodded, and pointed to her chest with a bony finger.

'You?' said Jen, frowning. Claire's heart sank. Where on earth was this all going?

Andrew bustled back in with a heavily laden tray. 'Now then,' he said, putting it down on a low coffee table in the centre of the room. He was about to begin pouring the tea when he noticed that his mother was jabbing herself repeatedly in the chest.

'Andrew, I'm sorry, but I'm not sure what your mother is trying to tell us,' Claire said.

'Oh,' he said with a smile, still holding the teapot. He raised his voice. 'She's telling you that she's a direct descendant of Katherine and David's brother, John Hume , isn't that right, Mother?' Mrs Ross beamed. 'We both are, obviously,' he added.

'That's wonderful,' said Jen.

'Yes. Now, let me get this right,' said Andrew, still shouting. 'Katherine Hume is Mother's great-, great-, great-, great-aunt.' He counted the fingers on his left hand. 'That's right, isn't it, Mother?' He lowered his voice to a more normal level. 'I've maybe got that wrong. So many greats. But you get the idea. It was a long time ago, of course. And I suppose you could add in the same number of "greats" for David Hume too. Just swap in "uncle",' he said with a chuckle. 'I just add another "great" for myself.' He began pouring some weak tea into bone china mugs. 'We couldn't believe it when we saw you on the TV talking about Katherine Hume and suggesting that she painted that picture, the one of the skater.'

He passed round the mugs and offered them some French Fancies.

'But that's not all,' he said, hauling himself back up to standing. 'There's more,' he added conspiratorially. He carried a mug of tea with a straw and a plate with an unwrapped cake to his mother and placed them carefully on a side table to her left. Then he reached over to the sideboard and picked the top book from a neat stack of three. They all appeared to be very old, and Claire could see that the pages were wrinkled together in tight curves and the spines were tatty and worn.

'These are Katherine's actual diaries,' he said triumphantly. 'Written in the last ten years of her life, or something like that. We've had them in our family since then.'

He held the book out to Claire, who was at that very moment taking a bite of her French Fancy. She popped the rest of the cake into her mouth and quickly wiped her sticky fingers as surreptitiously as possible on her jeans, then reached out to take the book.

'I think you might find them rather useful,' Andrew said. 'They just sit on our bookshelf forgotten about. But then we saw you on the news and Mother got very excited. I gather you've been wanting some more information about Katherine Hume and her life. So what a bit of luck we were watching!'

'It's just extraordinary,' said Claire, through a mouthful of cake.

'You have no idea how thrilling this is,' added Jen, leaning in to Claire for a closer look at the book.

'Well,' said Andrew. 'I think you'll be interested. I had a quick glance at one of them this morning. I have to admit, it's not something I've ever actually read from cover to cover, but Mother has, I think, though perhaps not for a long time. The handwriting is rather difficult to make out and it's faded a little, but you might have some luck with it. I hope it will help you with your research.'

Mrs Ross nodded once more.

'It most certainly will,' said Jen.

'It was so good of you to take the trouble to contact me,' said Claire, staring in awe at the book. She was about to open it when the old lady began to make a gurgling noise.

'What's that, Mother?' said Andrew.

She was clearly attempting to say something. She waved frantically at Claire, beckoning her over, and Claire stood up and moved closer to her chair, holding the book out towards her. The old lady began pointing frantically at it with her left hand. Claire wasn't quite sure what to do.

'The diary? Do you want this diary?' she said, still holding the book out. 'Or one of the other ones?'

Mrs Ross shook her head. Then she tapped repeatedly on the cover. It seemed painfully difficult for her to get any words out. She moved her lips but nothing could be heard. Claire looked to Andrew for some suggestion as to how to proceed.

'Now, Mother,' he said. 'Dr Sharp has the diary now. You don't need to get agitated any more.'

But still the old lady tapped on the cover. She became increasingly frustrated at being unable to communicate what she wanted to say until with a wild wave of her left hand she swept her mug and plate on to the floor with a clatter.

'Oh dear!' said Andrew. He dashed out of the room while Claire handed the book over to Jen so she could pick everything up. Andrew came back in with a cloth and began mopping up the tea.

Mrs Ross still looked upset. She had a hand on her cheek, and her face was strained. Andrew patted her knee. 'It's all right, Mother,' he said. 'These things happen. Don't worry about a thing.'

The old lady seemed utterly exhausted, but she looked over to Claire and fixed her with a watery gaze. She pointed once more at the little book, still in Jen's hands, and this time pressed her left hand to her heart.

'Oh,' said Andrew. 'Now this I do understand. Love. She means love.'

'You love the diary?' suggested Jen.

The old lady shook her head.

'Well, she does,' said Andrew, 'but actually, I think if I remember correctly the last bit of the final diary, the last little book there, is all about love.' He raised his voice again. It sounded as though he were making an announcement. 'She was in love with some chap, isn't that right, Mother?'

The old woman nodded keenly.

'That's who she writes about, I believe not long before she actually died,' continued Andrew. 'Katherine, you see, was head over heels in love with a gentleman called Pringle.'

Chapter 41

Claire rested the precious diaries on her lap as they headed back to Edinburgh.

She hardly dared touch the little objects. She almost felt she should be wearing some of those white cotton gloves archivists used when handling hallowed artefacts.

Despite her protestations, Andrew Ross and his mother had insisted that she take the diaries away so that she and Jen could spend some time looking at them; the writing was so small and elaborate, Andrew had explained, it would probably need close examination with a magnifying glass. The Rosses had also been quite adamant that any information or evidence the women found relating to the painting could be used for their own research. Mrs Ross in particular had been quite insistent in her agreement of this.

Claire couldn't get over the wonder of it all – the connection, and the coincidence that they had seen her on the news. Perhaps all the online abuse had been worth it to retrieve this rose from amongst the thorns. She found she was tingling with the sheer exhilaration of it all. She and Jen had seen the caricature of Pringle with Katherine, so they knew there was at the very least a friendship, and the discovery that Katherine was in love with him fitted perfectly with their hunch that the painting of the skater was an act of adoration. It was love poetry in oils.

'I don't think I can wait,' said Claire loudly over the noise of the car engine. 'Can we stop somewhere to look at them? Now?' She glanced over to Jen.

Jen laughed. 'You don't need to shout any more.'

'Oh. Sorry. My throat is actually sore from all that shouting at Mrs Ross, poor thing.'

'I think I know the perfect place to stop,' she said. 'But we'll maybe lay off the fish and chips for now?'

Claire gave a little gasp. 'Yes! I've got sticky French Fancy fingers!'

'Don't think I didn't notice you giving them a wee wipe on your jeans,' said Jen.

Claire smiled. 'I should really carry a pair of white gloves in my bag.'

Back in the city, Jen turned in to Holyrood Park.

'Where are you taking me?' Claire asked.

'Duddingston Loch. Seems a fitting place to go, no? Seeing as we're passing.'

'What an absolutely perfect idea,' she said.

They parked the car in a small car park circled by cherry trees in full blossom, and wandered across the road to the path that led down to the lochside. The sky was a blanket of unending blue, and apart from a mother and toddler looking at the ducks all was quiet and peaceful. They found a bench and looked out over the water, framed by the canopy of oak and beech trees.

'I've not been here since I was a child,' said Claire. 'I'd forgotten how beautiful it is.'

'Must've been lovely in the winter, all frozen solid,' Jen agreed.

Claire drew a breath. 'Right. Shall we? I'm assuming we should focus for now on the final one?'

Jen nodded.

Very carefully, Claire opened the pages. Katherine's writing was exquisite – neat, uniform, with very few corrections. The ink was a rich brown, almost black in places, and she made distinctive loops for the letter 'd'. Each entry was short, sometimes just a few lines, but she had interlaced them with fascinating little doodles and drawings. Claire began at the beginning, reading aloud, very slowly as she deciphered the writing.

'Tonight my brother and I made a very splendid new

acquaintance, Mr Francis Pringle, a distant cousin from the Scottish Borders who has arrived to take up residence in my brother's flat in James Court. What a very fine gentleman! He has impressed us all with his wit and good humour. He is a writer of poetry and has already made quite the impression on our circle of literary friends. He dined with us here in the New Town but we expect to see him a great deal. He has what I would describe as a most pleasing countenance, jovial and also quite lacking in that most common of male attributes: conceit!'

Jen laughed. 'I like her already,' she said.

Claire turned the page.

'I called upon Mr Pringle very early this morning, along with our dear friend the actor Mr Samuel Foote. Mr Pringle was delighted to see us. He yearns to join the Edinburgh Skating Club! As the weather has turned bitterly cold and icy, we suggested that Mr Pringle might like to practise on St Margaret's Loch. Mr Pringle held my hand and quite depended on me as he took his first steps on to the frozen loch. He took to it extraordinarily well and within no time at all found his balance.'

'Oh! what a merry evening we have had!' Claire continued. *'My brother, Mr Pringle and I attended a most comical play at the Theatre Royal. It was called* Taste *and was a most diverting and entertaining performance. We dined afterwards with the star actor himself, our very own Mr Samuel Foote, who played Lady Pentweazel. He is quite the clown! What a merry party we were. Mr Pringle made mention of my skin, which he said glowed with radiance in the candlelight.'*

'Oh my,' said Jen. 'She's already rather keen on him, I feel. How old was she at this point in her life, I wonder?'

'Well, in those caricatures she wasn't a young woman, was she?'

'Yes, she and Pringle definitely looked older. Around our age, perhaps?' Jen gave Claire a nudge.

'You read a bit now,' Claire told her, handing over the diary. 'It's hard-going on the old peepers.'

Jen took the book and fished for the glasses on a beaded chain around her neck. She placed them on her nose and flicked through the pages, scanning as she went, focusing intensely on the tiny writing in front of her.

'*Mr Pringle and I spent a most pleasant afternoon walking in the new gardens in Princes Street. We took dear Foxey and met many fine, courteous friends and acquaintances. Mr Pringle was a most attentive companion. He actually took the time to ask if I were feeling the cold and if he could return to the house to fetch my fur stole. Such care and attention!*'

Jen turned the page. 'Blah, blah, blah . . . oh, listen to this . . . *Mr Pringle and I took a journey today together in the carriage to Cramond. There we attended the kirk and took luncheon with the good minister, the Reverend Robert Walker and his family.*'

Claire let out a gasp. 'What? Not the Reverend Robert Walker? This can't be real!'

'*We met him one early morning, skating,*' Jen continued.

'He and Mr Pringle have become firm friends, and I with Mrs Robert Walker. We will, of course, invite them to dine with us here in town. Their children are a delight.'

Claire shook her head in disbelief, while Jen flicked on a few pages.

'It is remarkable to me how Mr Pringle worries. He is making such excellent progress, but he cannot see it. Oh, how he frets and complains. But now he must take a great leap! This is no jest, for he must learn to jump. Three hats! I found a laddie who was curling at Lochend, a boy called Squirrel, and I've said I'll pay him if he can get Mr Pringle to leap into the air on our next outing to Duddingston.'

Claire let out a chuckle. 'Oh, this is wonderful,' she said. 'And it happened right here.' They both looked out at the water and took a moment to take in their surroundings before Jen continued to read.

'I do believe skating quite becomes Mr Pringle. He has such a fine posture that he looks rather magnificent. He skates now as though it were quite the most natural thing in the world. Soon, I have no doubt, he will be a proud member of the Edinburgh Skating Club and wear that medal he so yearns for. Oh! But now how he complains of his aches and pains! I say to him, "Mr Pringle, you are quite the most terrible child the way you do wail and moan!" This does lift the mist and then he laughs. I think that Mr Pringle quite depends on me.'

'Well, that confirms his skating credentials,' said Claire.

'Ah, now, just wait a second,' said Jen. 'I think we've found what we're looking for.'

'What?' said Claire.

Jen passed over the little book. There were doodles, in ink, at the foot of the open page: one of the curve of a leg, wearing skates; another a foot on the ice, the last of a leg outstretched.

Claire stared in disbelief. 'Oh my God!' she said. She realised there were tears in her eyes. 'I don't know if it's definitive proof, but . . .' She flipped over the page and there was another doodle, this time of a hat, the same hat as in the painting, and the profile of a face. It had been repeated over and over again, all across the page.

'Well, well,' she said quietly. She peered closely at the tiny drawings. 'This is just . . . everything, Jen. What an incredible discovery.'

'Obsessive,' said Jen, with a smile.

Chapter 42

As the sun had begun to dip to the side of the loch it had taken with it any warmth there was to offer on this late spring afternoon, so Claire and Jen set off back into the city. Jen came up to Claire's flat and they sat with a pot of tea at the kitchen table while Claire read aloud the rest of the diary. This time she had taken Andrew Ross's advice and held a magnifying glass that she fortuitously found in a drawer in her kitchen to examine the writing.

'Mr Pringle and I attended the Caledonian Ball at the Assembly Rooms. It was a most refined evening. And we were, if I may say, quite the most elegant couple in the room. We led the dancing with a Minuet and I sensed the ladies present were quite envious of me. Mr Pringle took my hand and we walked out in front of everyone. I even overheard a tête-à-tête between the Smeatons agreeing that we were a most exquisite couple. I

do confess my heart is quite taken.'

'Well, things are getting quite serious. What next? An engagement?' said Jen.

Claire flicked over the page. 'Hmm. It would seem not,' she said. 'Listen to this. *I do declare that, along with my dear brother, Mr Pringle has gone. I believe my heart has shattered, for what other explanation can there be for this terrible ache in my chest? No such sorrow was ever felt. There were never so many tears shed as from these eyes. I have lost so much in so little time. My heart knows not how to be. He hath made a most distressing exit.'*

'Ah,' said Jen. 'Of course. All references to Pringle, in my research, did seem to stop quite suddenly, so that fits very neatly.'

'So you were right: he did disappear, and by the sounds of it he was presumed dead. I'm assuming she's referring to her brother's death here.'

Jen nodded. 'It sounds like it, doesn't it? Poor Katherine, her beau gone at the same time her brother dies.'

Claire flicked through the rest of the book. There were just empty pages. 'That's the end.'

'Really? How unsatisfying not to know what happened.'

Claire put the book down with a sigh and refilled their tea cups.

'It's all just a bit too perfect, though, isn't it?' she mused, lifting her cup. She took a sip. 'The love story, I mean. It's as if one of those Instagram filters has been applied to it.'

'And, I suppose crucially, we're only hearing one side of the story,' added Jen.

Claire frowned. 'Yes, that's true. But the story we're hearing is almost like a romantic novel written by a lovestruck teenage girl, not a woman in middle age.'

Jen nodded. 'It appears our Katherine felt it all very deeply. Perhaps it was the first time she had ever been in love. We can only hope for her sake that it wasn't un-requited, and that Pringle did die, rather than reject her.'

'Yes, that would have been the lesser grief, I guess,' conceded Claire. 'But it's still tragic.'

She absent-mindedly began leafing through the pages and running her fingers over the outside cover of the book. As she reached the last page, she realised that the end paper on the back cover was loose. It felt as though something had been tucked carefully under it.

She slipped her fingers inside the open flap and very carefully extracted a thin, folded piece of paper. She opened it up and out dropped a dark coil of hair, tied carefully with a fine piece of ribbon.

'Ah!' said Jen. 'Pringle's hair, maybe? A lover's memento.'

'And this looks like a letter,' said Claire, looking at the unfolded page. The hand was the same as the diary, with identical whirls and loops, but this time there was pressure in the pencraft. The ink had left blobs and there were corrections, words scored out. The scratchings of her quill had been pressed deep into the paper, leaving it wrinkled and fragile. There seemed to be intense emotion in this outpouring, even anger. It wasn't easy to decipher the words and Claire had to inspect it very carefully. She began to read aloud, slowly.

Dear Mrs Cockburn,

Forgive me, dearest friend, for I am full of remorse. The words I uttered on our last meeting were said in vexation. I am fatigued with grief, my spirit depressed, and I know not how to be.

I return to you this lock of hair, the purpose of which was for my portrait of you skating on Duddingston Loch. That painting is with Mr Raeburn at his studio. His apprentice was to alter the hat, which as you know was not to my satisfaction.

I cannot bear to look upon the painting again. Please tell Mr Raeburn to destroy it, or dispose of it in whatever way he sees fit.

I cannot think of Mr Pringle without weeping. I do so wish I had never set eyes on him; that you, Mrs Cockburn, had never become him, for you did it too well! He bewitched me most cruelly. It was our 'Twelfth Night': you Viola, who dressed as Cesario, and I your unwitting Olivia. And in that great play, Viola says: 'O time, thou must untangle this, not I. It is too hard a knot for me t'untie.'

From Pringle, I must hope that time allows me to untangle my heart.

I ache for you that your son Adam has returned and is so distressed with our little endeavour. O, such sadness is upon us!

I cannot see you again, my dear friend. In truth, my heart cannot bear it. I shall grieve quietly and alone.

Yours,

Katherine

Jen and Claire sat in silence for some time. 'Well, now,' said Jen finally, 'we didn't expect that, did we?'

Claire slowly shook her head. 'I can't believe it.'

'Alison Cockburn dressed as Francis Pringle?' said Jen. 'Wow.'

'She must have been very convincing,' said Claire. 'Too convincing, by the sound of things. She put Katherine into a spin.'

'So now we know why Pringle vanished so suddenly,' said Jen. 'Alison's son found out.'

Claire rested her chin on her hand. 'I'm in shock,' she said quietly. A moment later she sat up. 'Hang on, though – she never sent it. The letter. It was tucked away, hidden, in the diary. So the painting . . . the painting must have remained with Raeburn.'

'Presumably,' said Jen. 'So what happened?'

'I guess it was probably just absorbed into his own work.'

'Over time, and after his death no one would remember.'

Claire nodded. 'Or one of his apprentices took ownership of it, or something like that. But assumed it was a Raeburn and assumed it was Reverend Robert Walker. And then it was given to Walker's wife on his death. The rest is history.'

'It's the most incredible story.'

'Tragic too,' Claire added.

'Not a happy love story.'

'You know, I think Mrs Ross knew, and that's what she was trying to tell us when she was tapping the book.'

'Yes, of course,' said Jen. 'I wonder why she's never told anyone before. I mean, it's absolutely amazing stuff. And why did they not see that the sketches were so like the painting in the National Gallery?'

'Maybe she did; maybe they just didn't want to reveal the whole story,' said Claire. 'I mean, it's possibly because she's from a time when this would have been shocking. Not so much now, but I just wonder if it was something of a family secret, and now Mrs Ross and her son maybe are ready to let the world know the truth. When you think about it, it's a bit of a forbidden love story.

Possibly too shocking for even Mrs Ross in her younger days. But she seems to want us to know now.'

'Yep, she most definitely does.'

Claire began to smile slowly. Then she started to chuckle until she broke out into a hysterical laugh.

'What on earth is so funny?' said Jen. 'Have you lost it? Has it all got the better of you?'

'I'm just imagining Brian's face,' Claire said between great heaving giggles.

At this Jen too began to smile. 'Er, Brian,' she put her hand to her ear as an imaginary phone, 'guess what? That painting, ken the one of a man skating, painted by another man . . .'

'Well, it wasnae painted by a man,' continued Claire, 'and actually it's no' of a man at all, it's of a woman dressed as a man.'

'Stick that in yer pipe and smoke it!' Jen now too was red in the face, and tears were rolling down her cheeks.

'Oh, I can't wait,' said Claire, slamming her hand on the table in triumph. '*I cannot wait!*'

Chapter 43

18th century, Edinburgh

It was one of those bright, crisp, late January Edinburgh mornings. But Alison Cockburn's spirits could not be raised, even by her beloved city.

She was standing by the side of Duddingston Loch watching her fellow members of the Edinburgh Skating Club gliding gracefully around the ice. Oh, what she would have given to join them. She was, she thought, experiencing an intense form of melancholy. A sense of grief. She was mourning her friend David, whose grave she had visited to explain to him her absence from his funeral. She had also told his cold headstone of her distress at everything she had put their dear Katherine through. The guilt she felt for not having been there in his final hours, nor supporting Katherine in his final moments, was so visceral, it made her feel quite ill.

Furthermore, she felt utterly bereft at the loss of her companionship with Katherine. Her once most ardent supporter and closest confidante simply refused to see her. She had heard that Katherine was housebound now and gravely ill, yet she returned all Alison's correspondence unopened and would not see a soul.

Thrown into this misery was the confusion and indeed ache she felt at the loss of her identity as Francis Pringle. Being Pringle had unlocked the most wonderful phase of her life. She missed so much about that man. She allowed a tiny smile to spread across her face as she remembered. There had been innumerable wonderful moments, and the sense of camaraderie she had experienced was extraordinary. But now of course, like Pringle himself, it had simply evaporated.

As she stood there, the Reverend Robert Walker skated past her. He did not know her, and yet she had dined in his house, with his family, with Katherine at her side only weeks ago.

Turning to walk away from the loch, she happened upon Mr Foote, looking dapper in a rich velvet coat.

'My dear Mrs Cockburn,' he said, tapping his hand to his hat. 'To see you here, well, has quite made my day.'

'Mr Foote,' said Alison. 'How are you?'

'Do you know, it is most fortuitous that I have met you here? I was planning to call upon you.'

'Oh? For what purpose?'

'Will you walk with me, my dear?'

'Of course,' said Alison. He put out an arm for her, which felt strange and yet comforting, and they began to wind their way slowly back towards town.

'I have arranged for a delivery to your house,' he said. 'You remember that vile little oaf Smellie, don't you?'

Alison smiled. 'Oh yes, I remember him.'

'He has a costume that is rightfully yours, my dear.'

'A costume?' she said with a frown. 'I'm assuming you are not talking about that mantua dress, Mr Foote, but the masculine garments I wore as Francis Pringle, in which case I do not want them. Our little social experiment led to nothing but the cruellest heartache and devastation.'

Foote raised a hand to wag a finger. 'Tush,' he said. 'It wasn't all bad, now, was it? There were moments of great pleasure and wonder. For us all! You are a talented actor, my dear. And sometimes, we actors find a role that is our pièce de résistance!' He stopped and turned to her. 'For me, it was Lear, for Smellie it was the Fool. For you, dearest, it was Francis Pringle. Your performance was a triumph!'

Had it been 'a performance'? considered Alison. Had it not in fact been her true self?

Then his face became serious. He held both of her hands. 'Katherine is not well, my dear. The strain took its toll, perhaps . . . I fear it won't be long.'

Alison nodded, her eyes brimming with tears.

'Now it is time for the final encore,' said Foote. 'For you both.'

Chapter 44

21st century, Edinburgh

'How many times have we looked at this painting, and yet not really seen it?' said Claire. 'I see so much more now than I ever used to, even as an art historian.'

Jen nodded. They were standing once more in the National Gallery in front of the painting labelled 'The Skating Minister'. 'You could say that about almost everything,' she said. 'Every painting, every building, every piece of social history, is just that. It's really about the people behind it.'

'And even the people themselves,' said Claire. 'Do we really know them?'

Jen smiled. 'Exactly.'

'What we present to the world and who we truly are are such very different things,' said Claire. 'The secrets, the hidden truths, the human spirit in all its flawed and vital forms.'

'I wonder, do you see anything about this figure to suggest it's a woman dressed as a man?'

'I think we are seeing exactly whom Katherine saw when she looked at Francis Pringle. We are seeing the man she fell in love with. To her he was perfection.'

'Indeed he was. Well now, are you ready for this?' Jen looped her arm through Claire's.

'I am,' said Claire.

They turned and began to walk through the galleries towards the hidden corridors of offices that dwelt within the bowels of the building. They were here for a meeting with the senior management to present to them the information and evidence they had collated, including those precious diaries.

'It might not be the easiest path, and I can see there will be much unpleasantness hurled our way when the news is unleashed to the world,' said Claire. 'But it's the truth. We are doing this for Katherine Hume, for Alison Cockburn and for all those brilliant women who have been forgotten, who were unrecognised, who were not allowed to excel or flourish in their era.'

'For the Women's Enlightenment,' added Jen. 'In the past, in the present and for the women of the future.'

'And for love!' said Claire. 'Wonderful, unexpected, all-consuming love in all its forms.'

Epilogue

'Madam, can you hear me?'

At first, the whispered voice was distant. It was as though she were in an enormous ballroom, and the voice coming from the far end. Was she dreaming?

'Sorry to wake you, madam, but you have a visitor.'

Katherine decided that this was not a dream but a real voice. She slowly opened her eyes. The lids felt heavy, and it took a great deal of effort to focus on the face in front of her. The flicker of the candle flames cast shadows, and the eyes she stared into seemed to dance with light.

But then she recognised the heart-shaped face of Peggy. She remembered where she was, lying in bed in a darkened room with the heavy drapes drawn. Peggy was kneeling beside the bed, her hand resting on her mistress's shoulder, her expression all concern and agitation.

'You have a visitor,' she repeated.

'What time is it, Peggy?'

'It's just gone five o'clock, madam.'

Foxey, who was nestled on the bed, stood up and stretched and then circled back to cosy in to his mistress once more.

'It's black as night,' muttered Katherine.

'That's January for you, madam,' answered Peggy, straightening the blanket that lay rumpled over the bed. 'Madam, Mr Pringle is here to see you.'

At the mention of his name Katherine drew in a tight, laboured breath.

'Mr Pringle?' she murmured slowly, her brows knitting together. 'Can it be?'

Peggy nodded. 'Yes, madam. He's in the parlour. He wants to see you. He's asked if he can come and visit you in your bedchamber.'

'Prop me up, Peggy,' said Katherine in a whisper. 'And fix my cap and hair.'

'If you're sure, madam,' Peggy said, tenderly lifting Katherine's shoulders and head until they rested against the plumped pillows, then straightening her nightcap so that her hair hung in neat ringlets.

'Pass me my looking glass,' Katherine said quietly.

Peggy handed over the mirror. Katherine stared at her reflection and then lifted a bony hand and squeezed her cheeks so that tiny spots of red appeared on the translucent skin.

'You look quite beautiful, madam,' said Peggy, taking back the mirror.

Katherine smiled and patted Peggy's hand gently. 'I am ready.'

Peggy nodded and slipped out of the room.

Katherine felt the pace of her heart quicken; her breathing became quite rapid. There were footsteps on the floor outside the bedroom and then the door opened. Oh, to see his face once more! The thrill spread over her like an unstoppable wave. He was wearing a hat, which he now took off before walking towards the bed, an arm outstretched. Foxey looked up and wagged his tail.

'Katherine, my dearest,' Pringle said, and crouched by the bed, his face close to hers.

'Francis,' said Katherine, her voice laboured, her breathing tight and strained. 'Is it really you? I thought I should never see you again.'

'Ah, my love,' said Francis. 'Now, whatever made you think that?' He took her hands in his and squeezed them tight.

'You look so handsome,' said Katherine. She felt the softness of his velvet coat, and smelled the smoky Edinburgh air which hung on his skin and clothes. 'Francis, I'm not sure I'm going to manage it, you know,' she whispered.

'Manage what, my dearest?'

'Duddingston, to see you skate again.'

'Nonsense,' said Francis. 'I shall bundle you up in furs and rugs and we shall take a fine carriage together. And I shall skate, and you will sketch, and we shall be happy once more.'

Katherine smiled. 'We did have such lovely times, did we not, Francis?'

'The happiest,' said Francis. 'The very best of times.'

Katherine's eyes were suddenly wet with tears and she gripped Francis's hand. Foxey whined and nestled into his mistress.

'I'm so sorry for everything I said,' Katherine sobbed, her words barely audible.

Francis shook his head. 'Don't distress yourself, and don't apologise, please. You must not get upset.'

'I just became lost in it all,' said Katherine. Her breathing became a wheezing sob. 'It consumed me. Like nothing I have ever known. First infatuation, and then the deepest, deepest love.'

Francis gripped her hand. 'We both got lost, we both felt those things, we both became something quite, quite different. But wasn't it wonderful too? As you said, what is life without adventures?'

'To feel love.' Katherine said the words she had kept clamped tightly in her chest for so long. 'I have loved you with all my heart, Francis.'

Francis wiped the tears from her face. 'Dearest,' he

said, 'I must ask you something. Something really quite important.'

'Anything,' said Katherine. 'Anything for you, Francis.'

'Do you think, in the spring, you might consider becoming my wife?' He paused. 'Because you must know I love you so very deeply too.'

Katherine's sobs became laughter, and Francis laughed with her, their heads bowed together.

'We could get married in the kirk in Cramond,' he whispered. 'On a bright spring day when bluebells carpet the ground. And then we could take a walk by the sea . . .'

' . . . watch the boats sailing on the Forth,' whispered Katherine. Her energy was beginning to fade. She lay back fully on the pillow, allowing her head to sink into the softness. The tears on her cheeks rolled into her hair. 'And honeymoon in the Isles?' she murmured.

'Of course. What do you say, Katherine? Will you?'

'There is nothing I would like more,' said Katherine, with all the energy left in her failing body, 'than to be yours, Francis Pringle. You are, quite simply, the most wonderful man I have ever known.'

Francis leaned in and kissed her forehead. Then Katherine closed her eyes, and once more she and Francis were dancing, in the Assembly Rooms, by the flicker of candlelight, all eyes upon them.

What a handsome couple they were . . .

'. . . there is nothing so pleasant and wholesome to the human heart as to love and be loved.'

Alison Cockburn

Author's Note

Alison Cockburn, 1712-1794, was born in the Scottish Borders. She was, by all accounts, a gregarious, witty and mischievous individual. Regarded as a 'literary hostess', she held soirées and literary gatherings in her flat in Edinburgh's Crichton Street, and was described warmly by those who knew her.

A great letter writer, she corresponded regularly with David Hume, whom she teased rather beautifully. She was a distant cousin of the mother of Sir Walter Scott, and met the great novelist as well as many other Enlightenment celebrities of the day, including Burns, Rousseau and Dr Johnson.

She herself was a writer. Her most famous work is considered to be the ballad *The Flowers of the Forest*, published in 1765 and hailed by Robert Burns as 'a charming poem'. See 'A Group of Scottish Women' on the Electric Scotland website – a useful resource, with a page devoted to the life of Alison Cockburn.

For further reading on Alison Cockburn's life, in *The Sewanee Review* an article by Winifred Snow, written in 1905, is a lovely read.

If you can get hold of it, the book *The Social Life of Scotland in the Eighteenth Century* by Henry Grey Graham has a chapter, 'Town Life in Edinburgh', that gives a detailed and glorious insight into life in Auld Reikie in the 1700s. I found it hugely useful for my research and Mrs Cockburn is referenced several times.

But as to the events of this book: did Alison Cockburn dress as a man? Did she and Katherine Hume 'create' Francis Pringle? And did Katherine Hume capture her dear friend skating on Duddingston Loch in that famous painting that hangs in the National Gallery in Edinburgh?

Perhaps, just perhaps . . .

Michelle Sloan
May 2022

Acknowledgements

A huge debt of thanks goes to my mother Kay MacIntyre and my sister Karen Smith, for whom I wrote this book. For their careful and enthusiastic reading, I am extremely grateful.

I would also like to mention and thank my father, Alasdair MacIntyre, who used to take me for childhood walks down the Royal Mile. We would wander up and down the narrow closes and his knowledge of historical Edinburgh was encyclopaedic. He took me to the National Gallery, too, where we would gaze upon the Skating Minister.

Thanks also to Viccy Coltman, for her time in answering my more obscure art history questions, Polygon editor Alison Rae for her encouragement and enthusiasm for the project in its infancy, and also my wonderful copy-editor Nancy Webber.

And finally, thank you to my family for always giving me a life full of adventures.